Tony Johnston

# THE MUMMY'S MOTHER

*The Blue Sky Press*

AN IMPRINT OF SCHOLASTIC INC. • NEW YORK

My heartfelt thanks to Kasia Szpakowska, Ph.D.,
University of Wales Swansea, author of
*Behind Closed Eyes: Dreams and Nightmares in Ancient Egypt*,
for her steadfast help with this book: Praise be!

THE BLUE SKY PRESS

For information regarding permission, please write to: Permissions
Department, Scholastic Inc., 557 Broadway, New York, New York 10012.
SCHOLASTIC, THE BLUE SKY PRESS, and associated logos are
trademarks and/or registered trademarks of Scholastic Inc.
Library of Congress catalog card number: 2001043631
ISBN 0-439-32462-9
10  9  8  7  6  5  4  3  2          05  06  07
Printed in the United States of America      37
First printing, October 2003

FOR THE FAMILY!

# CONTENTS

# I

# GRAVE ROBBERS

"Got the Old Prune, Sid?" asked the grave robber.

"Yeah, Buster."

"Then let's go!"

"Mighta been a looker in her time," Sid said. "Now she's like—Shrivel City."

"Hey, you bozo, wrap 'er back up and close that thing!"

"Nuts to you, Buster! Ya don't got no historical interest."

Sid covered the face he'd been sneaking a peek at and clapped the coffin lid shut. Grunting, the two crooks hoisted the bulky box to their shoulders. They left the unwieldy marble sarcophagus behind.

"Shake a leg!" Buster yelled. "Those museum boys are waiting in port!"

"I'll hurry all right," Sid griped, "if this wormy old queen's casket don't slip and squash me."

Suddenly, another voice pierced the dark like a flute: *"Son, they are stealing me! Help!"*

The mummy had been listening from his secret space inside the wall of the tomb. He was ten years old, or had been at the time of his demise, when he was visited upon, unfortunately, by a plague. Now he was four thousand and ten, approximately.

Many people had searched for the mummy family over many years. So the mummy had come to know many languages. English, Arabic, Icelandic. He knew exactly what was happening.

"Mother!" he called in panic.

No answer.

For ages the mummy and his mother had lain in the tomb, waiting for the Afterlife (which was taking an *awfully* long time). They rested close together—she in the open; he sealed up, conversing pleasantly about this and that. Or just enjoying the quiet. Never in all that time had she failed to answer him.

Too well he knew the reason for her silence: His mother was gone!

"Thieves! Pirates! Plunderers! Pillagers! Pilferers! Purloiners of mothers!" the mummy boy shouted, but only the cold walls heard him.

This was a crime to spur any son to action. Without analyzing exactly how, grunting and pushing against a concealed door, he suddenly found himself outside his hidden chamber, wobbling a lot, woozy from lying down for forty centuries—and woozy from losing his mother.

Heartbroken, he flung himself down upon the spot where she had been and sobbed himself sick.

After a while, the mummy stopped crying. He had no tears left. To gather himself, he took a deep breath.

The tomb smelled of must and mold and mice, which was nice. All was quiet. Still as stone. Suddenly—*heep! heep! heep!*—small chirps echoed in the limestone room.

The mummy was so frightened, he nearly shrieked. But then he realized *he* was causing the sound. He was hiccupping.

"I wish Father were here," he said aloud. "He would know what to do."

But his father was plastered up in a faraway tomb, so cunningly concealed, perhaps no one would ever find him.

The mummy whispered to himself nervously, "Ramose, you alone can save Mother. You must *do* something—quickly."

Ramose pondered several plans.

"Let me see. I could wish upon a scarab, become Horus the falcon, track the villains down, claw their eyes out, and retrieve Mother. Or—I could wish upon a scarab, become Sekhmet the lionness, bound up behind the thieves, shred them to smithereens, and retrieve Mother. Or—I could wish upon a scarab, become Anubis the jackal, tackle the scoundrels, bind them with mummy cloth, and retrieve Mother. Or—"

Just then, words from long ago entered his head: *Son, never leave to chance what is yours to be done.*

The mummy interrupted himself. "Be realistic, Ramose. Mother was right. Waiting for magic is a very weak plan; you must rely upon yourself."

Ramose felt pretty stiff. Quickly, he did some stretches to limber up. He was about to depart when he froze in his tracks. In all his life he had never ventured anywhere by himself. A servant or other trusted household member had always been his constant companion. After all, he was nearly a king.

*How can I do this alone?* he wondered, so worried he could not move.

But each moment he hesitated, the farther away his mother was getting. With that in mind, Ramose gave chase to the grave robbers, calling upon every god he could think of to guide his bandaged feet.

His eyes were accustomed to dark, so he stumped along with ease, through the mazed tunnels, past gorgeous funerary reliefs, up a steep ramp, into the resplendent sun.

Too resplendent.

*"Aghk!"* Ramose gasped. After the cool embrace of the tomb, the desert heat, enough to bake an eel, nearly knocked him down. He reeled, but stood firm.

Frantically, Ramose looked for clues to follow, but the sand had already swallowed the culprits' footprints. Which way? Desperately, he tried to decide, but he found himself reflecting instead upon his mother. She was not much older than he, with a gentle voice and eyes that were lovely, dark, and deep. She had been a good queen, and good to him. To be snatched from her last resting place by burglars was an indignity no one deserved, especially not his mother. How was she? *Where* was she? He had no inkling.

"I forbid you to cry," he commanded himself.

But he was only a frightened little boy, so he cried anyway.

Something nudged him. A large and unattractive beast, hanging around outside the slabby mastaba that housed the tomb.

"What are *you*?" Ramose screeched.

"A camel," the animal snorted. "Where've you been all your life?"

"Mostly in a tomb," Ramose explained. "There were no camels when I was young." Ramose marveled. He could not recall speaking with animals as a boy. A lot can happen in four thousand years!

"No camels! What a world!" The camel sneered. "Say, why're you crying? You tourists just can't take the heat."

"I am not a tourist," Ramose replied. "I do not even know what a tourist is. I am a mummy. A famous one."

"Har! Har! Har!" The camel spit in the sand. "Yeah, and I'm a famous hippopotamus."

"This is a very grave matter! Thieves have made off with my mother! Haste! We must pursue them at once!"

"What makes you think I want any part in this?"

Ramose's head swam. "She is a *mother*! She must be saved!"

"I never liked my mother much," the camel remarked. "If it were *my* mother, I'd give 'em a good head start. By the way, where're they headed?"

Ramose bit his lip and tried to think. *What had Buster the grave robber said? Those museum boys are waiting—*

"In port!" Ramose cried, delighted with this recollection.

"What's a port?" asked the camel, suspicious.

"A place of boats."

"Near the sea?"

Ramose was so desperate, he jumped up and down and kicked the sand in a most unkingly way.

"Naturally!"

"Don't get all unraveled," snapped the camel. "Any water there?" His nostrils trembled at the thought.

Ramose well knew that seawater was salt. He felt a twinge of guilt, but it was a clear choice—this nasty camel or his mother.

"The whole place is afloat!" he screamed, neglecting to mention the salt. "Take me to the nearest port!" Then, just in case, he added, "Uh—please."

"Oh, all right," grumped the camel. "I've never seen the sea."

With cameloid grace, he sank down, front first. Ramose scrambled atop him, and then with a grunt the creature lurched to his feet. In a heaving lope, they were off.

Ramose yelled as loudly as he could, *"I'm coming, Mother!"*

# I I

# HOT PURSUIT

RAMOSE was in hot pursuit of his mother. The hottest pursuit imaginable, for the eye of the sun glared down upon him most wickedly. This dry place, the Red Land, as it was known, was little but daunting dunes, stretching endlessly in all directions, like the beastly hot humps of countless gigantic camels.

To the boy's great distress, almost at once, the camel became bored with the monotonous landscape and slowed down. He dawdled as much as possible, or so it seemed. The only time he perked up was when they passed a thorn bush or some other kind of pricker, which he ate at once.

*No wonder he has such a prickly personality,* thought Ramose.

Sometimes the camel snuffled the air, most likely for signs of water. Sometimes he wandered off on a bizarre new course.

Once they passed a charming oasis. From a spring, the camel guzzled greedily. The place was comprised of the trickle of water and a cluster of palm trees. Ramose loved palms. Their rough, dark bark and their graceful green fronds reminded him of beautiful old men beneath feathered canopies long ago.

"Are we still heading to sea?" he asked anxiously.

"Huh?" replied the camel stupidly, as if sizzling from sunstroke. But his head was too hard for that. He enjoyed tormenting Ramose.

They pressed on, looping hither and yon. At last these meanderings became just too much.

"Do not wander! Do not graze! Keep the pace! *Faster! Faster!*" Ramose commanded. The words flew from his mouth like ugly toads. He was astonished that he was able to muster such harsh language.

The camel swiveled his head around. "What do you take me for," he sneered, "a racehorse?" With that, he plunked down.

"End of the line," he announced. "I decline to go on. I refuse."

Ramose was horrorized by this behavior. He heartily wished to jump down and kick the brute with all his might. *But kings do not kick camels*, Ramose thought. *They let their servants do that.*

Besides, he knew that his bones were quite brittle. He did not dare kick even a pillow. He might pulverize himself with one blow. Furthermore, this much was clear: The more sullen the camel, the slower he went. When—and if—Ramose struggled his way into port, his mother would most certainly be gone. He needed to rouse this creature!

"Get up!"

"Not a chance!"

"*Arise, beast!*"

"Never! Even if another oasis lush with date palms and cool sweet water springs up before me this instant!"

"You do not mean that!"

"Whatever I mean, *you* will be the last in the world to know!"

Panic gripped Ramose. He stammered, "M-m-my f-father would l-lop off your head for this!"

"Do you see him anywhere around?" the camel asked sarcastically.

"Well, no," Ramose admitted.

Ramose was not a bloodthirsty boy. Even if he had possessed the proper tools, he knew he could not lop off anybody's head. He was too kind. And he knew nothing of the technique. How did one even begin lopping? Besides, as the saying went: A headless camel is a useless camel.

*I wish I had more experience!* he thought. But, unfortunately, he did not.

"All right," said Ramose, giving in. "I will do anything you ask, only *please* keep going."

"Anything?"

"Anything."

"OK, take this dratted saddle off," said the camel. "And these saddlebags. The whole contraption rubs like crazy and gives me calluses."

Ramose had expected a far more complicated request. "All right," he agreed, then quickly added,

"—as soon as we reach port." He was surprised and pleased that he had thought of that.

"Promise?"

"I promise."

"One more thing," snapped the camel. "I have a name, and I'll thank you to use it."

"Of course. What is it?"

"Mahmut."

Even a near-king's promise is binding. The bargain was struck. Mahmut arose and strode on. He quickly picked up speed, moving with such ease, Ramose got the odd feeling that he himself had become part of a light wind billowing over the sand.

He relaxed. He stopped worrying about Mahmut's direction or eating habits. Instead, he looked up and reflected upon Re, the sun god. How many centuries had it been since he had seen his glowing face, felt his long fingers warm his skin? In the heat of the moment, he thought of a poem, awkward but heartfelt:

> Dear Sun, old Sun,
> older even, than I am.
> I missed you in the tomb.
> Thanks for warming me again.

Ramose liked his poem. He repeated it once or twice, changing some words to make it better.

"Mahmut," he called, "what do you think of this poem?" He recited it with feeling.

"It's stupid. Why give thanks for being baked alive?" remarked Mahmut, spitting vigorously. "You could spend your time better looking for your mother."

How frivolous of him, reciting verse when his mother was lost! Ramose was embarrassed, most of all because a rude camel was the one to point this out.

From then on, Ramose fixed his eyes upon the sand, searching for clues—footprints, bits of clothing, anything. His mother was a clear thinker. Being a dead queen, she was overloaded with jewelry, too. So, given the opportunity, she might fling an amulet or shabti figurine or golden ring onto the sand, to leave a kind of shining trail to follow. So far, nothing. But hope fluttered inside him like a small bird.

As they climbed a particularly steep dune, Ramose spied a patch of white at the crest. It was not another thorn bush, unless one had been bleached and had sprouted feet or wings. For whatever the thing was, it was moving, bobbing in the blazing breeze.

*Goodness, me!* Ramose thought, imagining many dangers.

He squinted to better see—a turban. And it was not alone. It was wrapped around somebody's head!

Ramose's throat clenched as tight as a fist. What if it were one of the grave robbers? Or both? Or a whole horde of thieving scoundrels? What if they dashed down now and filched *him?*

"Crikey!" grumbled Mahmut. "Is that one of your famous thieves coming?"

"We—shall—soon—see," Ramose squeaked, so scared his voice trembled like an off-key flute. He tried hard to act calm and kingly, but the hollows inside of him churned.

For what seemed forever, Ramose watched the person materialize beneath the turban as he came closer and closer. With each step of the man's sandaled feet, grainy shots of hot sand spurted out, for he was running, bearing down upon them.

The figure was a bedouin, a nomad of the sands, garbed in a dark kaftan, carrying a very large bundle under one arm. A bundle the size of a mother.

The stranger's eyes glittered like a desert snake's.

"Praise be for this most fine day!" The bedouin greeted them loudly in a singsong way.

"Praise be!" replied Ramose, most politely—and most suspiciously.

"Praise be for this most fine mummy!"

He seemed oblivious to all but the business at hand, including Ramose's wrappings.

Greatly pleased with his merchandise, the bedouin grinned slyly and shoved the parcel under Ramose's nose. "Want to buy it?" he wheedled.

"Maybe," said Ramose. "I *am* seeking a mummy."

"Excellent. The price—one stereo set."

"I do not understand," Ramose said. He had never heard of a stereo set.

"Clearly, you are not from around here!" bellowed the bedouin. "I speak of a most marvelous noisemaker."

"You speak *like* a most marvelous noisemaker," remarked Mahmut under his breath.

Ramose replied to the bedouin uncertainly, "Well, should this be the mummy I search for, perhaps I could find you such an item. But first," he suggested timidly, "may I see your wares?"

The bedouin's eyebrows rose slightly. He clutched the thing more tightly.

What if he changed his mind and stalked away with his mother? Ramose was worried.

"OK, small boy." The bedouin grinned like a brilliant slice of moon. He boomed, "Come see this most fine mummy!"

Suddenly and wildly the small hope-bird battered inside Ramose's rib cage so that he could barely breathe. Shaking all over, he slid from the saddle and down to the sand.

"Don't get your hopes up about your precious mother," said Mahmut sourly. "I bet my front teeth it's a fake."

Unaware, the bedouin salesman cried, "Feast your eyes on this! My mummy is top quality."

Ramose gently touched the wrappings and whispered with tenderness, *"Mother?"*

# III

# LOST

RAMOSE trembled all over like a loose harp string. The mummy before him could be his very own mother. With great care he began to unwind the linen cloth about its face.

There was dead silence. Eagerly, Mahmut and the bedouin leaned close. So close, Ramose could smell their rancid breath.

Ramose whispered a small prayer: *"In the name of all goodness, please be my mother."*

He already had a pretty good idea that this was not—even before he saw the cartouche that ringed its royal name. To ease his fears, *his* mother would have identified herself at once.

When Ramose saw the mummy's face, he knew the worst—he was unwrapping a total stranger.

He was so embarrassed, he blushed.

"Praise be! A beauty. A classic in the true sense," cried the bedouin enthusiastically. "You cannot pass this by."

"I can," Ramose replied sadly. "This is not my mother."

"Nor mine either," replied the bedouin, surprised.

"I cannot purchase a stranger," said Ramose with heavy heart. "Onward, Mahmut!"

The bedouin leaped to his feet. *"Impossible!"* he railed, furious at the loss of a sale.

But there was nothing he could do. Ramose and Mahmut left him fuming in the sand, shaking his fists at them and shouting, "You will regret not making this most fine purchase! A lost opportunity! LAST CHANCE TO SHOP!"

"Told you so," Mahmut told Ramose in a withering way, when they had gained some distance.

Ramose made no reply, too disappointed to speak.

They proceeded on their way. Mahmut moved gracefully, nearly floating over the sand, as if lofted by a desert wind. A lovely sight, considering his awkward appearance. Too bad there was no one to admire his gait. But for them, the desert was deserted.

Now and then Mahmut lifted his head, perhaps to sniff the stifling air for water. Perhaps to snuffle out the great port they were seeking. Once his nostrils flapped loudly. But if he smelled anything of interest, Mahmut revealed no hint of it.

Ramose did not ask. *The beast is far too touchy,* he thought.

Constantly searching the sands with his gaze, Ramose hoped for a clue to where his mother had gone.

Nothing. Not a trace. Not a signal. Not a sign.

He slumped in the saddle as a horrible thought struck him. He might be alone forever, searching for his mother. He would never give up. He loved her. Besides, his father, wherever he was, would expect nothing less of him. Ramose was a would-be king!

Suddenly, he looked down and saw a wink of

blue in the sand, like an eyeball. Maybe it *was* an eyeball! The desert holds many wonders.

"Over there!" Ramose commanded, excited once again. "See?"

"I don't see anything but grit," Mahmut remarked acidly. "What is it?"

"An eye, I believe."

"Oh, *marvelous*," Mahmut sneered. "There's nothing more appetizing than an old eye."

But a beggar accepts what gifts come his way. As they approached, Mahmut bent to nibble the object with his large loose lips.

"Stop!" Ramose spoke so sharply he surprised himself. The words just blurted forth, for he recognized the thing. It was one of his mother's beads, painted with a delicate black lotus design. He slid down with haste and picked up the bead, tenderly turning it in his hand. Through its smooth, faience crust, he could almost feel her presence.

"Mother has passed this way!"

"Who cares, for pity's sake? She's just a dried-up old sack!" snorted Mahmut with spite, having lost the chance for a snack.

*"She is leaving me a trail to follow!"* Ramose cried.

Leaping once more onto Mahmut's mountainous back, he yelled eagerly, "Onward!" He could not wait to find the next bead.

But Mahmut could. His pace slowed and slowed and slowed. Worse yet, he shifted completely around.

Ramose was frantic.

*"What are you doing?"* he yelled.

"You're starving me. I'm going back."

"It is one tiny bead! Camels do not eat beads!"

Mahmut sniffed haughtily. "You think you know everything! You're nothing but a junior mummy—not exactly an expert on eating! Anyway," he declared, "I have absolutely no interest in finding more jewelry. And I have changed my mind. I do not wish to see the sea."

"Keep going—please!" begged Ramose.

Mahmut pretended to be deaf as a sphinx. He plodded back—toward where they had begun.

Ramose was too flabbergasted to speak. He had no idea what to do. He had never felt less like a king. But if he did not do something, his mother would be forever lost to him.

At that thought, Ramose quivered all over, but he overcame his fears. He bent and whispered into Mahmut's ear, "Remember those saddlebags, cutting into your tender flesh? Take me to that port, or I will load them down with sand. Then you will see what *real* calluses are."

Mahmut sneered, "Sand, schmand. That's already been done by the wind."

"Well—rocks, then!"

"Rocks, pox! There's not one single rock within miles."

"There are fossilized clams."

It was true. They were scattered everywhere, like large, gray ostrich eggs.

Angrily, Mahmut kicked a big clam at least six feet into the air. He spit like he had never spit before.

"This is the dumbest thing I ever heard of!" he fumed. "Chasing your mother across a flame-hot desert! She probably ran away on purpose!" he added in a highly offensive tone. "Ever consider that?"

Ramose hadn't. He believed his mother loved him, just as he loved her. It was a reciprocal thing.

But now Mahmut was casting doubt upon their very relationship.

"But she called out to me when they took her away!" Ramose protested.

"To notify you she was leaving. A courtesy."

"She left me a bead in the sand!"

"It fell—by accident."

*"Stop saying those things!"* Ramose plugged his ears and hummed to block out the sound. But he could hear Mahmut making miserable suggestions all the same. He was only a boy, four thousand ten years old, in the middle of a blazing desert with a foul-tempered camel, who was making rotten remarks about his mother (a queen, no less!). What in the world could be worse?

"Halt!" he said, too confused and upset to go on. "We are staying here tonight."

Heavy with sadness, Ramose got down and tied the camel rope to a wizened bush. Neither spoke. They just lay down and looked up, waiting for the stars to fill the sky, as they always did. Then they fell asleep.

———

At daybreak Ramose learned what could be worse than the previous day's predicament. During the night, Mahmut had gnawed through his rope and vanished, saddlebags and all. Ramose was lost in the Red Land, and he was alone.

# IV

# THE MOST FINE SEA

RAMOSE had no idea where he was. Just stranded somewhere in the midst of the shifting, drifting desert. He had relied upon Mahmut's large and water-sensitive nose to lead them to the sea, to where Ramose's mother surely was. But in a temper fit, Mahmut had run off. He wished the beast were with him still. Enduring peevishness was better than enduring loneliness.

"Oh, my goodness. It's blistering hot here." The heat made Ramose gasp. Beneath his sweaty bindings, he itched horribly, but his bulky hands could not scratch.

"What if I shrivel up and die?"

Then he remembered—*that* had already happened. This memory lapse made him smile briefly. But he became depressed once more.

"I cannot do this alone," Ramose told the silent air. "I am but a boy—an old one. I have no experience in searching for stolen mothers. I need guidance. From a father. A best friend. Perhaps Thoth."

Thoth, the wise, was his favorite god, in part because of his earthly form, an ibis with a curved beak like a rind of dark moon.

On the offhand chance that the god might be near, Ramose spoke aloud: "Oh, mighty Thoth, if you are anywhere around, kindly show me a simple sign—nothing fancy. Or send me a good idea."

He waited eagerly, but nothing happened—except that the sun rose higher and hotter.

The desert is a secretive place, holding many dangers and many mysteries. By night it is vaulted by the great arc of stars; by day the sand is grand. It is a place to raise the spirit—and to crush it in an instant.

"I am stranded," Ramose said abruptly. "Mother is lost. Perhaps I should give up."

In this moment he heard his mother's voice, as if she sat beside him: *The smallest heart can display the largest courage.*

Though feeling frightened and hopeless indeed, Ramose tried to be brave. "I will go on," he resolved.

He hesitated, not knowing which way to step. If his choice were wrong, he would be going away from his mother. Like the hand of a confused sundial throwing shadows willy-nilly, he gingerly took steps in all four main directions, and many in between, unable to make a decision. His hands clenched. His nerves became utterly frazzled.

Luckily, just then he glanced down and noticed a glint, a gleam.

"*Oh, let it be!*" he prayed.

"Mother's bracelet!" he shouted.

Ramose stooped to scoop up the glimmering object.

"Jusssst what do you think you're doing?" a thin voice hissed as a slim head poked up right through the center of the bangle. "That'sss *mine.*"

Ramose jumped back, startled, upon seeing the reptilian apparition. For a time, he could only stare at the snake before him, feeling too jangled to speak. Its eyes glittered brightly like shards of stars. Its flickering tongue licked the hot air nonstop.

"It is *not* y-y-yours!" Ramose managed to stammer at last. "My-my mother left it for m-m-me. She has been abducted, and I am following the bejeweled trail she is leaving."

"Let me get thisss ssstraight," said the snake venomously. "Your mother, a victim of foul play, ssselected thisss ssspot in the midsssst of thisss immenssse desert and tosssed a sssmall bracelet down, knowing full well that her sssharp-eyed ssson would come ssstrolling along and ssspot it."

"She *did*! Well—sort of."

"Well, thisss isss the firssst sssuch item to come my way, and I do not intend to losssse it. Essspecially not to the likesss of a sssswaddled child."

Ramose ignored that remark.

"But I *must* have it!" he screamed. "It is all I have by which to remember her!"

"What isss the matter with your brain that requiresss a bracelet to trigger it?" asked the snake. "Can't you recall your mother with utmosssst filial sssweetnesss whenever you wisssh?"

"I do not think I have a brain anymore."

"Graciousss! The talesss jussst grow taller and taller."

"*It is the truth! I am a mummy!*"

"Oh, for heaven'sss sssnakes!"

"I *am!*"

"Then how do you think?"

"I have no idea."

The snake began swaying, rising inside the bracelet, grazing the metal in a papery whisper with its dry, pebbly skin.

"Sssuch a lovely piece," it hissed. "Worked from sssilver, with lapisss lazuli and carnelian encrussstationsss, ssshaped like a butterfly. A collector'sss item, sssurely. And it'sssssss *mine.*"

The snake, with its covetous turn of mind, was driving Ramose crazy. Its movements were beginning to entrance him. He had to do something to recover the bracelet. It was part of his family, part of him.

There came a sudden stillness.

"No sssmart sssstuntsss," hissed the snake. "Or I ssshall ssstrike you, and you will expire inssstantly from my poisssonsss."

"It is too late for that," Ramose replied, his head wildly working on a way to seize the bangle.

"Don't try anything, or I will ssssqueeze you. And you and your rotten wrapsssss will become nothing but dussst, and you will never recover your mother. You will sssimply be blown away over the sssandsss by sssoft-breathed windsss."

The snake's tone made it clear that it greatly enjoyed that concept.

Ramose, on the other hand, hated it. Being squashed to dust would mark the end of his quest.

"You are not of the squeezing species," he declared, though utterly unsure of that.

"Yesss, I am."

"No, you are not."

The snake's eyes smouldered. It smiled. "Care to tessst that theory?"

What would his father do? Ramose knew. By now, he would have snatched up the reptile and snapped it like a whip, forcing its head to bid farewell to its tail.

But Ramose could not hurt a flea. Besides, if he tried, he might become mummy powder.

Ramose was terrified. He shook so, he worried that his teeth might pop out. But he *must* have the bracelet for a keepsake, since he might never recover his mother.

In a blink, quick as a jackal, Ramose lunged with his left arm, grabbed with his right, then jumped back as far and as fast as possible. In the same split second, the snake sprang like a great hissing worm. Goodness, it was quick!

But not quick enough. Ramose had escaped—with the precious bracelet!

He was astounded by his unexpected success.

*How did that happen?* he wondered.

Tears pricked his eyes as he slipped on the bracelet. Then Ramose lumbered off with such speed, the snake could not keep up.

As he went, his eyes raked the dunes feverishly for more maternal signs. There—twenty paces ahead—a bead! And another! And another! It was as if his mother herself were a lovely necklace coming unstrung.

The jeweled path led Ramose over sand and sand to—wonder of wonders—the sea! As he stood on the vast, gritty lip of a dune, he saw its great blueness in the distance, spreading out like wide blue shimmering hands.

"That wretch Mahmut knew we were close!"

What did that matter now? Ramose was so exuberant, he danced about. He felt like a reed filled with lovely notes, which again and again he sang with delight: "Praise be for this most fine sea!"

Then he began running as fast as he could, following the trail of jewels, down to the vast and shining sea. Down, he hoped, to his mother.

# V

# THE COFFIN TAKES A TRIP

RAMOSE emerged from the desert, dazed, amazed, astounded, stunned, and utterly staggered by the sight of the sea! Forty centuries ago there were boats here, to be sure. Graceful and slender, but few in number. Now the whole place teemed with white boats that floated upon the water like bloated gulls. They bristled with masts, masts, masts, poking into the great blue sky like needles. There were larger vessels, too. Some as tall as sandstone cliffs, it seemed, and as grand.

And the smells! Of tar and oils and unknown fumes. And pelicans and terns and gulls. And mullet and bream and eels. And ropes and rust and rats. And bales and bundles and boxes. And fishing nets that reminded him of his mother's openwork raiments. And wafting everywhere was the pleasingly pungent perfume of the Great Salt Sea. That, above all, Ramose recalled from when he was a living boy. Suddenly, he missed life. With the sharpness of a fishhook, the thought stabbed him in the deep-down place of his heart.

He stood at the edge of a great path that was heavily and darkly plastered, like a wide swath of tar. Along its length, instead of the carts pulled by donkeys that he had always known, strange and shining monsters of many colors swept by at a fantastic pace, uttering deranged and high-pitched screeches.

By now, Ramose's bindings bulged with a varied collection of his mother's trinkets. For in his desert travel, whenever he had discovered a bit of her jewelry, he had stuffed it safely inside his tatters. He was certain that he looked ridiculously lumpy, but he did not care one whit.

Just then he saw another hunk of something, about the size of a fig, shimmering beyond the path.

"Mother's prized greenstone scarab!"

Ramose *had* to reach it!

*Honk! Honk! Honk!* The crazed creatures blasted out, paralyzing him. He stood, poised to take a step. But he simply could not move.

"What is it, my dear? Are you ill?"

A voice spoke kindly into his ear. He turned to see an old woman beside him, thick and squat and stooped, carrying a large basket with squids slopping over its sides. Most probably he should not speak with her, for she was a stranger. But he was quite unable to resist. She reeked of onions, a dear smell from his childhood.

"How did you guess that something was wrong?" Ramose asked.

"For one thing, you are heavily bandaged," replied the wise old woman. "For another, I have given birth to seventeen children. I have had some experience, my dear. So now, where does it hurt?"

"Oh, nothing hurts," replied Ramose. "But I cannot move."

The old woman peered into his hollow eyes. She poked at his ribs, but they were too well wrapped to feel. She touched his forehead, testing, no doubt, for fever. She tried to pinch, gently, the flesh of his face. All the while she was making this examination, she clucked, "Tut-tut-tut."

"I am no doctor, just a mother," she confided to Ramose. "But my guess is you suffer from lack of water. You are the driest boy I have ever seen."

"I have been in the desert for quite some time," Ramose explained.

"Hot squid soup. That is what you need. Come home with me, and I will make you some."

"Thank you," replied Ramose, "but I feel fine. I need no soup. What I require is my mother."

The old woman gazed into some far-off place. "At times, we all need our mothers. . . ."

"Mine was stolen, and I am trying to find her."

"Stealing mothers! In my time, thieves were a higher class of people," the old woman remarked indignantly.

Her kindness had calmed Ramose enough that he could tell his tale.

"My mother is leaving a trail for me to follow," he revealed. "That green bulge over there is her scarab."

He pointed. She squinted.

"Please, help me cross this great path," Ramose pleaded. "I am frightened of these flying beasts."

"How sensible," remarked the woman. "You must be from the country," she added.

"Mmmm," replied Ramose, not wishing to lie.

"The path is a street, and those beasts are cars." Then she said, "Come with me."

Gathering up her basket, she stepped into the street, head high, one hand raised in some sort of signal.

The big honkers understood. On all sides they screeched to a halt. Calmly, the old woman navigated the street like a little boat. Ramose clutched her arm, his eyes riveted on the scarab.

"That is the bravest thing I have ever witnessed," Ramose remarked when they were safe. "Are you a queen?"

The old woman laughed. "Not that I know of."

"But you are fearless, and you walk like one—like my mother," Ramose said sadly.

"She must be proud of you."

"I doubt it," replied Ramose. "I have never done much."

Luckily, the scarab was still there. Other people had not noticed it. They were too busy to look down. Ramose crouched and picked it up. Once more he felt his mother's closeness.

"Here," Ramose said in a spurt of emotion. "I give this scarab to you."

"A big bug. How nice," remarked the old woman. "But I could not take it. It is your mother's."

"I have other reminders. Please. She would want it so."

"Thank you. You have a generous spirit." The old woman glanced at the squids slumped in her basket. "Dear, dear," she remarked. "I must get my little friends home. No soup?" she asked again.

"No soup."

"Good-bye, dear boy. Good luck."

"Good-bye. I will not forget you."

As they parted, Ramose looked up at a monstrously large and mastless ship. On one flank was painted H.M.S. *Gigantic*. Many people were packed upon the top deck, leaning over the rail, chattering and squawking and waving like flapping gulls.

As he admired this marvelous bulk, Ramose noticed two men lumbering up the boarding ramp. They were hunched over, sweating and straining under the weight of what they were lugging—a large and colorful box—his mother's coffin!

Up and up and up they lurched until they reached the top. Then they vanished from view.

A sound like a great ram's horn mourned so loud and deep, it made the ground beneath Ramose's feet shiver. Way up where the two men had been, people waved wildly and yelled, "Farewell! So long! Good-bye!"

The monster boat was leaving!

Ramose ran, faster than he had ever run in his whole life. All the while, he sobbed and wailed, "Wait!"

# VI

# SWALLOWED BY A SNAKE

"Out of my way! Stand back!" Ramose yelled, completely forgetting his manners.

Carefully, on account of his crumbly condition, he pushed and shoved and thrust aside everybody he met. When he reached the ship's ramp, he used equal delicacy to hustle his way to the top.

He looked around frantically. The coffin was nowhere in sight. He paused to catch his breath. The sun beat so hot, he felt he might melt.

"Are you sweating, Pansy?" a whiskered man asked the lady beside him.

"Copiously."

A steward all in white was directing things.

Ramose very much liked what the steward was wearing. He liked what everybody was wearing, for the passengers were dressed up in a very grand way, in floaty fabrics and complicated headdresses.

Ramose glanced down at himself. By this time he looked pretty ratty. He wished that he were clad in a pleated white kilt for this occasion, trimmed perhaps in peacock blue. He wished he had his golden sandals. And a spreading collar of precious stones. And an adornment for his sidelock. He wished. . . .

Suddenly he remembered his mother. He stopped thinking about clothing.

Ramose was frightened by the steward. The man seemed far too crisp and stern. The mummy stirred up his courage.

"Excuse me, sir," Ramose asked timidly. "Did you see a big box go by?"

"Please, little boy, run along. I am welcoming the arrivals."

"I am an arrival."

"Welcome," said the steward. "Now run along."

Ramose had no idea which way to run. He very much wanted to cry. Fortunately, the sweaty, whiskered man smiled and said, "That way." And he pointed. The sweaty lady waved at Ramose.

"One thousand thanks!"

Ramose stumped down the deck, peering around the people and their belongings, trying to glimpse his mother's coffin. After a while, he made a marvelous discovery—a door, which many people were entering. Ramose entered, too. He found himself on a staircase that wound down and down and down.

Soon Ramose was deep in the bowels of the ship. It had stairways and corridors and passages that crisscrossed like the insides of his tomb. But nothing else was the same. There was not a splash of color. Not a glyph from the pyramid texts. Nor the star-studded heavens painted upon the ceiling above. Everything blazed white and blank.

Ramose felt blank. And frightened to the bone. Nothing about this world was familiar, except that it was quiet. All the people had vanished.

*Prink! Prink! Prink!* Ramose was startled by a

sound. His spirits lifted. Somebody was tapping. He pricked his ears like a desert deer.

*Prink! Prink! Prink!*

"Mother! She is sending me a signal!"

He followed the taps on tiptoe, so as not to muffle them. He was close. Oh, close. He turned a corner and saw a wondrously long and large white snake, perfectly round, stretched along the wall. It did not move. Ramose felt terribly uneasy, for he could not see its head. At any moment it might attack.

Ramose had had enough of snakes. He wanted to run away. But the tapping continued.

He thought of his daring father, conquering people, slashing enemies with his sword. Should he survive for *fifty* centuries, Ramose could never have such courage. To the gods he entreated, "Oh, let me be just a little brave. Enough to save Mother."

*Prink! Prink! Prink!* The knocks were coming from inside the monster.

*"Mother has been swallowed!"*

Breathlessly, Ramose crept close and spoke, "Mother, are you in there?"

No reply. Of course, she was not there. How

would she fit? Whatever this object was, it had not swallowed anybody.

"How will I ever find her?" he wondered dismally.

Ramose found himself back where he had begun, motherless and alone. He sat down on a step and moaned, "I wish I were safely back in my tomb."

"What a weird wish," said somebody.

# VII

# BOYS

RAMOSE swung around. A boy about his age was looking at him, gripping something in one hand.

"Why are you talking to that steam pipe?" asked the boy.

"The what?"

"The pipe. The thing that's hissing on the wall."

"Oh. I thought that perhaps my mother was inside."

"That's a good one!" hooted the boy, collapsing in spasms of laughter.

"It is not funny," Ramose remarked. "It *could* have swallowed her."

"You are one weird kid," the boy replied. "What are you doing here?"

Ramose was sick to death of explaining his problem, but he said patiently, "I am seeking my mother, a queen. She was stolen. I must get her back to our tomb. What are *you* doing here?"

"In the big picture, I'm on a field trip with my school—a private one in New York—to learn about Egypt. By ship, to get the full-on ocean experience. Miss Brickface, our teacher, is with us. Miss B. tries not to let us out of her sight. We try to escape her. It's a little game. We call her The Hat."

This game, Escaping the Teacher, sounded like excellent fun. When he was a student, Ramose would have loved doing that.

"Why do you call her The Hat?"

"You'll see, when you meet her. Anyway, right now, I'm checking out the ship. Getting the lay of the land."

Ramose felt dizzy. None of this made sense.

"I do not understand. Checking out? Lay of the land?" They were now upon the water, after all.

The boy shot him a funny look.

"Say, who *are* you, anyway?"

"I am Ramose. I am a mummy."

The kid snorted. "Right, you're old King Tut, the merry old nut—"

He squinted at the trussed-up person before him and suddenly went bug-eyed.

"Jeez! You *are* a mummy! Now your outfit makes sense! I thought you'd been flattened by a truck. Wow! I can't wait to tell the guys!"

"Guys?"

"My friends."

Ramose had always wanted friends. Unfortunately, as an almost-pharaoh, he had spent most of his time in the company of grown-ups, learning how to rule.

"You have friends?" he asked longingly.

"Sure. I'll introduce you. By the way, my name's Gerald."

Ramose had countless questions to ask Gerald.

"What are you carrying?" he blurted. "Forgive m-m-my curiosity," he stammered. "This is all so new, and so terribly exciting."

"No sweat," replied Gerald. "It's a briefcase. For papers and stuff. I take it everywhere."

"You mean you have scrolls in there? Can you write? Are you a scribe?" Ramose asked a series of questions in rapid succession, totally awestruck. In his land, scribes knew a lot. They were much revered.

"Not exactly," replied Gerald. "I mean, I can write. But I'm just a plain student. Everybody studies in my land. Everybody writes like mad."

Ramose was too flabbergasted to speak. At last he inquired timidly, "Could I see something you wrote?"

"No problem." Gerald unzipped the briefcase and pulled out a page with scribbles on it.

Ramose gaped at the toothy zipper. He touched it. Gingerly, in case it nipped him. Then he touched the paper and the marks upon it.

"Do these have meaning?"

"My teachers don't seem to think so." Gerald giggled.

"Decipher them, please."

Gerald read the title with flair: "*A History of Egypt* by James Henry Breasted, Ph.D." Gerald explained to Ramose, "It's a book report."

"Oh, my goodness. I have never heard of a book."

"Jeez, man! You've got some catching up to do! Better read *The New York Times*, like me. Say, speaking of catching up, let's go find the guys. They've gotta meet you!"

"I have never met many boys," Ramose said anxiously. "Maybe they will not like me."

"They will. *Guaranteed.*"


Gerald knew the ship like the freckles on his hands. In no time at all, Ramose and Gerald found Gerald's friends. They were clustered by the rail, seeing who could spit farthest into the sea. The other passengers kept their distance from the boisterous group.

Ramose watched the boys. They seemed so lively and carefree. They were all dressed like Gerald, in short leg-coverings and colorful, loose overgarments. On their feet were what resembled grubby loaves of bread. One of the boys looked like a weird duck, for his headgear was pointing behind him. Ramose loved it at once.

"That glyph on his crown," Ramose whispered to Gerald. "Is it an amulet of protection?"

"Huh?"

Ramose pointed to the large NY.

"Oh, that stands for New York. The Yankees. Best team in the world."

"I would like such a crown," remarked Ramose wistfully.

"It's a baseball cap."

The boys stared at Gerald and his companion.

Ramose felt edgy. He wanted to bolt.

"Jeez!" one boy remarked to Ramose. "You're pretty banged up!"

"He's not banged up," explained Gerald. "He's a mummy. His name is Ramose, and he's four thousand and ten years old."

"Man! You've got *serious* age!" cried Morgan, amazed.

"His mother's been ripped off," Gerald added.

"No way, maguey!" the rest chorused.

"Yes, way!"

"Hey, can I sign your rags?" one boy asked blatantly.

"Certainly," Ramose replied in a friendly way, but shyly.

The boy grabbed a stylus—or something close— and wrote in huge curlicue letters: BRANDON.

Dissatisfied, he added a hieroglyph that showed an odd personage standing on a skinny wheeled board.

"This work of art is entitled 'Scooter Guy With Flowers Sprouting From His Ears,'" Brandon announced.

Everybody wanted to do the same — Morgan and Hunter and Quincy. Laughing, they passed around styluses of all colors, writing and drawing more and more wildly.

Soon Ramose was covered with lettering and illustrations.

"The Illustrated Man," Gerald remarked. "Sorry. They got carried away."

Ramose looked at himself, very pleased. "It looks perfectly marvelous!"

Boys *have signed me,* he thought happily. *I wonder what Father would think.*

"Say," asked Quincy, "how come you've got an accent?"

"A what?"

"You talk funny."

"I learned my English in the tomb. From British people trying to find me."

"I *say*!" cried Morgan.

"*Pip! Pip!*" shouted Hunter.

"Righty-*ho!*" yelled Quincy.

Gerald spouted a song:

> He learned his English in a tomb.
> British English, stiff as broom.
> He honed his diction to perfection
> in a moldy old classroom!

Everybody bellowed Gerald's ditty and cavorted like fools. Ramose chimed in. How long had it been since he had sung? He felt as joyful as a sparrow full of song.

"What we are doing?" Ramose asked. "What is it called?"

"Goofing off."

"This goofing off. How I do love it!"

It was the most fun he had experienced in four thousand years.

"Listen up, everybody," Gerald said suddenly. "Ramose has something real important to tell us."

Everybody huddled. Everybody listened intently.

"What am I to tell you?" Ramose whispered to Gerald.

"About your mother."

A bit flustered, Ramose began, "Yes. Well, then." He gathered his thoughts and plunged in. "Quite recently, grave robbers entered our burial chamber and, and as you say, 'ripped off' my mother. I followed the scoundrels to this very—uh—ship, where—"

"Well, well, well, what have we here?" Somebody interrupted the lively tale. A monster straw platter was perched upon her head.

Everybody leaped up and screamed, *"The Hat!"*

# VIII

# PING-PONG CHAMP

MISS Brickface stood there, arms akimbo, her grim little glasses glinting in the sun.

"What are you boys *doing*?"

She spoke so briskly that her straw hat quivered. Ramose shivered like a mirage. Miss Brickface seemed quite inflexible. Rather like his father.

*What if she lops my head off?* He was worried. *I will never find Mother.*

Gerald piped up, "We're discussing literature."

The word literature always had a positive effect on Miss Brickface. She placed high value on books.

"That's a blessing," she remarked. "I thought perhaps you were gambling."

"Never, Miss Brickface." Gerald laid it on thick. "This kid, Ramose, knows all the Egypt myths. We're picking his brain. We can't learn enough."

Gerald crossed his fingers. Ramose saw that. He guessed it meant that this was not a total lie, just a very bent truth. A myth.

"Well, hello there." Miss Brickface greeted Ramose, squinting to see him better. "Which school do you attend?"

Ramose felt so nervous, his mouth froze shut.

"Pharaoh's Academy," Gerald blurted. "It's a real old one."

"Isn't that nice. Interesting uniform," she remarked to Ramose. "Well, get back to that rousing tale."

Miss Brickface was leaving when she abruptly turned back.

"I almost forgot. I found this notice in my cabin."

She flurred a paper at them: *Ping-Pong tournament. Ages twelve and under. Sign up now. Win! Win! Win!*

"You boys will enter, I'm sure," said Miss Brickface. "Freddy Morrison Swinefest already has."

Brandon whispered, "Translation: Freddy Pig Party."

"You know what *that* means," Miss Brickface continued, ignoring the remark.

Everybody groaned.

"Man," moaned Gerald. "This stinks! It means our school, Ivy Wall Hall, has gotta challenge Pig Party's school, Old Ivy Wall Hall! Nuts to that!"

"Did I hear groans?"

"No, Miss Brickface."

"Did I hear desire?"

"Yes, Miss Brickface."

"Marvelous! The tournament begins in two days. Choose a whacking-good champion."

Chuckling at her Ping-Pong joke, Miss Brickface strode away at a crisp pace.

"We're dead," Gerald said. "Sorry, Ramose. No offense."

"What do you mean?" Ramose asked timidly. "Is Miss Brickface going to sacrifice you?"

"In a manner of speaking. Somebody has to play Ping-Pong against Freddy Pig Party."

"Is he an enemy?" asked Ramose.

"He's a braggart," said Hunter.

"He's a swaggart," cried Brandon.

"He's a gasbag," remarked Quincy.

"We're pretty klutzy," said Gerald. "He'll cream us. In public. It's the same as being sacrificed."

"Oh, my goodness."

"Say," Gerald said, gimletting Ramose with a look. "How good are *you* at games?"

Suddenly everybody was staring at him. Ramose felt overwhelmed. He closed his eyes and pretended the boys were not there. He opened them again. They were.

"Are you good at games?" Gerald repeated.

"I do not know," replied Ramose, remembering his childhood sadly.

"You are or you aren't. There's no in-between."

"I am afraid there is. When I was a boy, I was almost pharaoh. Everybody let me win everything."

Quincy pounced on that, "Ramose, you're a bona fide winner! You know the winning feeling!"

"You've got that winning feeling, woah, woah, *wooooooah.*" Gerald swooped around, mimicking a song he knew.

"Yeah," Brandon agreed. "Now all we've gotta do is teach you to play Ping-Pong."

The boys began to chant, *"Ramose! Ramose! He's our champ!"*

No one had ever cheered him before. Ramose felt a glow, as though a small sun were pulsing inside him, burnishing his every bone.

Then a horrible thought stunned him back to reality. "This goofing off has swept Mother from my mind!" he groaned. "What a useless, brainless son I am! I must go! I must find her!"

Ramose felt wobbly. Delirious. To have friends—true ones—was a thing he had dreamed of. Like beautiful flowers, these friends had sprung from nowhere. Now he would lose them. Now he was failing everybody—the boys, his mother, himself.

Aching inside, Ramose announced, most distressed, "I cannot be your champ."

# IX

# THE GREEN DOOR

"WHAT are you saying?" the boys chorused, aghast.

"He's saying, 'Don't count your champs before they're hatched,'" replied Gerald.

Ramose struggled to explain. "My mother is hidden somewhere on this ship. I must recover her and take her to Ta-Mery."

"What's that?" they all asked.

"The Beloved Land, our home. Then, together we may be transported to the Afterlife. In my realm, it is family first."

"Ditto for our realm," replied Brandon.

Gerald added, "She's not just any mother, she's a pharaoh-ess."

The boys gazed at Ramose with new respect.

"Man!" breathed Quincy. "You've got deep family issues!"

"Deeper than Ping-Pong," Morgan agreed.

"Oh, yeah, you *know* it," Hunter chimed in.

"Whoa-aaaa!" yelled Brandon. "To find a hot mummy stashed on this ship! What a *trip*!"

"Let's make a pact," Gerald said. "You play Ping-Pong against Pig Party, and we'll help track down your mother."

"No sweat!"

"No problemo!"

"Piece of cake!"

So this was friendship. Ramose was overcome. He said softly, "I most gratefully accept."

"Gimme five."

"Five what?" Ramose asked.

"Fingers, man. Smack hands. You know, to seal the deal."

Ramose did not know a thing about this ritual.

He glanced at his bandaged appendages. "I had better not," he remarked with trepidation.

"Good point," said Gerald. "They could easily crumble."

Gerald had a plan of the ship. He spread it open on the deck. Everybody hunkered down to check it out.

"We'll split up," Gerald announced. "To cover ground faster."

"Better buddy up," Quincy suggested, "in case of trouble."

"I pick Ramose," joked Brandon, "for my mummy-buddy."

Gerald glared. "Shut up, meatball. This is a family tragedy."

"Sorry."

Each pair got a section of the ship to comb. And a detailed description of the coffin. By this time, everybody was hopping up and down. They couldn't wait to take off.

Gerald felt that a motto was needed before they scattered. He yelled with gusto, *"Today the queen, tonight Ping-Pong!"*

———

The boys scoured the ship. They searched every nook and cranny. Every niche and recess. Every hole and cubbyhole.

Whenever a nosy passenger asked what they were doing, peering under deck chairs and stuff, they responded, "We lost our mother." The boys decided not to say what they were *really* after, in case other people wanted a mummy, too.

After a while, they met on deck. Everybody looked pretty glum. So far, no mummy. Nobody could think of where else to look, so they gave up and ate buffalo wings.

Ramose was despondent. His shoulders, his whole body, slumped.

"I am not clever enough to uncover my mother," he declared miserably. "I am—how do you say?—a surprise failure."

"That's a *prize* failure," Quincy corrected.

"Hey, we *all* failed, man. Don't be so tough on yourself," replied Gerald. "It ain't over till the fat lady sings."

"What are you talking about?" Ramose wanted to scream.

"It's a common expression. It means don't quit."

That night, the Ping-Pong lessons began. Or rather, the search for a practice room. They wanted to keep Ramose under wraps till he was ready, and then spring him on Freddy Pig Party. The whole bunch trooped around the ship, opening every door. Finally, they blundered on one nobody'd seen before. It was narrow. And green. Like spinach.

"How'd we miss this?"

"We're doofuses."

"I wonder what's in it," Quincy said.

"The Mystery of the Green Door." Brandon moaned the words out like a ghost.

Gerald turned the knob. Soundlessly, the door opened. In a peering pile, everybody leaned in. But the door was so slim, only Gerald had a view.

Ramose became light-headed with hope. He whispered, "What do you see?"

Gerald whispered mysteriously, "I see things— wonderful things."

Ramose whispered anxiously, "Is one of them my mother?"

# X

# FOLLOW THAT MUMMY!

GERALD told Ramose, "Take a peek."

Full of hope, Ramose crept up to see what secret the green door held.

The room was dim. Through the crack in the door, he saw a man in a tropical suit slumped upon a folding chair—snoring.

On the ground lay a long box. The man's feet were resting upon it. It was highly and gloriously decorated with figures and symbols and signs. The mask at one end was so thickly gilded, it shone. Two white eyes, outlined in kohl black, stared at the ceiling, from the mask of a face most beloved—his mother's.

Ramose felt a catch at the throat. He uttered no sound, but stared long and long, giving thanks.

At last he murmured, "Mother."

As if they had concocted an elaborate plan in advance, quickly and silently the boys went to work. The room grew so still, the only thing to be heard was their own breathing—and the mummy-sitter's snores. Like burglars, they tiptoed toward the coffin, two at the head, two at the feet. Gerald was lookout.

Lovingly, Ramose placed one hand upon the mask. If his mother knew he was close—surely she must—wisely she said nothing.

Ramose's knees were shaking. He knew what he must do. But all his old fears rose like a great blue roller upon the sea, nearly overwhelming him. He was only a boy. In a strange new world. Unlike his father, he had never accomplished a thing, other than dying. How could he possibly succeed? How could he free his mother without waking the guard?

To the god of nerves, should there be such a deity, he fervently prayed, "Great lord, hold me steady!"

Using utmost delicacy, as if lifting a cloud, Ramose raised the guard's feet.

With the swiftness of roaches rushing from light, the other boys slipped the coffin out from under and darted for the door. (Luckily, somebody had attached handles to its sides.) Ramose set down his burden, then, catlike, swiveled to follow. Unfortunately, in his eagerness, he stumbled, then righted himself and lurched out.

*Wham!* Gerald slammed the door and jammed it with his briefcase. "Beat it!" he yelled.

And they fled. From inside the room rose a banshee cry. "Help! Police! FBI! They've got my mummy!"

*Ha-hoooga! Ha-hoooga! Ha-hoooga!* Instantly, horns bellowed throughout the ship, as if somebody had been pitched overboard.

Hefting the coffin like ants with a twig, the boys scrambled through the labyrinth of passageways. They hustled as fast as they could, lugging their bulky cargo, amid the squeaks of the boys' new tennis shoes and Ramose's thuddy footfalls. Gerald barked out directions to keep them on track. People poked their heads out when they went by.

"Whatcha got there?"

"Need a hand?"

"Nice luggage."

Behind them came a clatter. A rising roar.

"Faster!" Gerald exhorted, craning behind him. "Posse's coming! I hear their thundering hooves!"

Everybody heard a rumbling roar: "FOLLOW THAT MUMMY!"

Struggling to the top deck, they looked for a place to stash the coffin.

Ramose was delighted with the rescue, but frustrated, too. His mother was so close, but he could not enjoy the reunion. He could not speak a word to her. Their pursuers were rushing the stairs!

"There!" Ramose pointed to a lifeboat.

With a burst of effort, quick as a school of sardines, they darted over and plopped the coffin inside. Ramose camouflaged it with a sail.

"Gum!" commanded Gerald.

He tossed everybody a piece. They ripped them open and chewed like crazy.

Ramose just held his. He did not know its purpose.

Pink bubbles soon bloomed from everybody's lips.

"What strange flowers," Ramose remarked. "It is magic."

"It's bubble gum," explained Gerald. "Everybody, look nonchalant. Here comes trouble."

Quickly, the group zipped away from the lifeboat and leaned against the ship's rail, blowing bubbles into the wind. At that moment, a band of people came panting up, as frantic as crazed baboons.

*Pop! Pop! Pop! Pop!* The people were greeted by wild pink bubble-gum explosions.

"Excuse me," said the former mummy-sitter, the leader of the gaggle and top-pursuer. "I am Dr. Smythe of the Central Museum of Art in New York City. Have you noticed anything out of the ordinary?"

His eyes were dull gray like the heads of nails, his build as robust as a hippopotamus.

"You mean weird?" Gerald replied.

"Exactly."

"Like what?

"A large bundle?"

"Nope."

"A strange crate?"

"Nope."

"A—er—coffin?"

"A *dolphin*?"

"A mummy box."

"Wow! What happened to it?"

"I—uh—misplaced it," stammered Dr. Smythe.

"Tough luck. Is it valuable?"

"Priceless. It is the mummy of a queen."

"Could be somebody's mother," remarked Gerald, in an offhand way.

For a moment, Dr. Smythe looked perplexed.

"Well, in any case," he said, recovering quickly, "have you boys seen it?"

Ramose was frightened out of his wits that he might be recognized. Still, for his family, he felt he must speak up.

Ramose replied, "Definitely, nope."

"Thank you, boys. You have been very helpful."

Dr. Smythe and his people swarmed the deck. Suddenly, Dr. Smythe spun around and came back.

He peered at Ramose.

"You look familiar," he said. "Don't I know you?"

Ramose thought he was going to faint. How could he have been so foolish—to risk all, to expose himself to danger? If only he had not been so sheltered a boy, he would have known better! Now Dr. Smythe was going to capture him, too! He and his mother would never again see their dear land. The Afterlife would be out of the question.

Just then, in a highly garbled way, he remembered Gerald's words: *It is not completed until the large woman warbles.*

*Do not quit,* he told himself.

Though as panic-stricken as a marsh hen at the approach of a crocodile, he strained to appear calm.

"You do not know me, sir," Ramose said, "but perhaps you know my mother."

Dr. Smythe scrutinized Ramose.

"My mistake. Forgive me. I must recover that mummy and escort her to New York! By the way, I would love to study the writings on your outfit some time. They are fascinating—especially that figure with flowers."

"Certainly," replied Ramose.

"Whew!" Quincy said, whistling when the men were out of range. "I was scared spitless!"

"Me, too!" everybody chimed in.

Ramose was amazed. He had thought he was the only frightened one. He was doubly amazed that he had been able to converse with Dr. Smythe without swooning.

"'Perhaps you know my mother'!" Morgan laughed. "Ramose, you are one cool customer!"

"Thank you?" said Ramose, uncertain of the correct reply.

"All *right*," Gerald said. "Score one for us; none for the museum. Hey, speaking of scoring, let's play some Pong."

"I cannot," replied Ramose. "I must go at once to Mother."

"Jeez! I'm such a meatball!" Gerald whacked himself in the head.

"Go, Ramose. We can practice real early in the game room," said Hunter. "We'll just sneak our secret weapon in and out before anybody else wakes up."

"What is this secret weapon?" asked Ramose.

"You."

Museum and ship officials were out of sight when Ramose and the boys headed toward the lifeboat.

"We won't hang around long." Gerald spoke for the group. "We just want to meet her."

"She will be pleased that I have friends," Ramose remarked with exuberance.

For the first time since the chase began, Ramose was about to speak with his mother. On the way over to her, he recited the words with which he would greet her: "Mother, I am here. Do not worry, I am taking you home."

But when he neared the lifeboat, Ramose felt a deep pang, like a blow in the belly from a large stone. He could not approach after all. Dr. Smythe was perched upon the edge of the lifeboat like an oversized seagull! The man was so close, he could have reached out and touched the coffin! Ramose felt a wail rising in his throat.

# XI

# AN UNUSUAL CHAIR

SOMEHOW, Ramose stifled the sound that was form-
ing inside him at the sight of Dr. Smythe sitting
upon the lifeboat-full-of-coffin.

"*Ohmygosh!*" exclaimed Brandon. "*He's so close,
she could bite him!*"

"I wish she would," replied Ramose. "Right where
he sits."

"Bummer," remarked Gerald. "You'd better come
with us. You can stay in my stateroom. It's first
class," he added, probably to cheer Ramose.

"Thank you," replied Ramose, completely cheerless.

Everybody figured Miss Brickface, a.k.a. The Hat, would be lying in wait for them like a spider. But she wasn't.

"Miss B.'s probably trying to sniff out mummies—with Dr. Smythe," Brandon remarked in a meaningful way.

"Yeah, I bet they're getting real chummy." Everybody giggled.

"Let's hope," said Gerald. "Then we won't have to sneak around so much."

Gerald's stateroom was nicely furnished, with a bed, a chair, a couch with tons of pillows, a desk, and a reading lamp. Curtains billowed at the window and wherever else the decorator had seen fit to hang some random yardage. The decor was in blues, all the colors of the sea. Jostling, the boys crammed in. Though Gerald had been its inhabitant for only one full day, it was already an appalling mess.

"Sit anyplace," he told everybody.

Ramose sat on a pile of dirty clothes sprinkled lavishly with peanut shells and pizza crusts.

Hunter was munching on something.

"What is that?" asked Ramose.

"Hershey bar," said Hunter, with his mouth full. "Wanna bite?"

"I do not eat."

"Oh, yeah. I forgot."

"A museum, please. What *is* it?" Ramose asked, extremely concerned and curious.

"A place full of cool old junk," Quincy explained, "like coins, suits of armor, dinosaur bones."

Gerald poked him. "Jeez, Quincy," he whispered, "don't sound so enthusiastic! That's where his mother's headed—and she's *not* junk!"

Quincy winced. "Sorry, no offense."

"What will become of my mother there?"

"She'll go on display," Morgan piped up.

"Display?"

"Probably in a glass case. So people can oogle her," said Morgan.

"You mean ogle?" Gerald asked.

"No, I mean oogle."

"What is glass? What is a case? What is oogle?" asked Ramose, extremely worried.

"You don't know much," remarked Quincy.

"Cool it, Quince!"

"It means view," Gerald explained. "Sorry to tell you, Ramose, but people will go to a museum like the Central to stare at your mother."

Ramose could not believe it! Before long, total strangers would be gaping at her—like a bear brought from far Retinu to his father's zoo! This was the lowest humiliation. And he was powerless to stop it, it seemed.

*"Why would a museum do such a thing?"* Ramose screamed.

"Obviously they forgot to consider the family angle," Morgan said.

"It's educational, I guess," said Gerald. "We'll check up on your mother for you. We practically live at the Central, thanks to The Hat."

"I cannot stand it!" Ramose crawled under the bed and refused to come out.

Slowly, the great sun disk of the god Re rose, like a beautiful blossom opening over the ocean. The water shimmered like the skin of a fish. Ramose was already on deck. Upon wakening under Gerald's bed, he had rushed back to the lifeboat to speak with his mother, only to find a sailor sitting upon her sail-swathed coffin, guzzling coffee. Unbelievable!

"Have they no other chair on this entire ship?" he muttered in utter frustration.

Ramose gazed out at the endless water, watching the sea's blue fingers ever and ever reaching. Never had he felt so helpless. He felt like a wave himself, reaching out for his mother, but grasping nothing.

*I am so close,* he thought, *yet I cannot manage even to speak with her. What a useless son I am. I have never before left the land of sand. Now I am going to a far place called New York City. How will I free Mother? How will we ever get home?*

Far below, upon the water, Ramose noticed a duck bobbing. He began sobbing.

At that moment, the boys appeared, bleary with sleep.

"Hey, man," Quincy greeted him. "How's your mom?"

"She is a chair," Ramose declared, overcome with gloom.

"Huh?"

"Somebody is sitting upon her."

"Bummer," everybody chorused.

"Hey," asked Gerald in a whisper, "why're you crying?"

"I saw a duck," replied Ramose.

"Good reason."

"When I was alive I loved to swim," explained Ramose. "Mother called me 'dear little duck.'"

"I get it, man," Gerald said sympathetically. "This may sound harsh, but wanna play Ping-Pong?" he asked. "Might take your mind off your mother."

"Our pact," said Ramose. "I completely forgot. Why not? Let us play this Ping-Pong. I will return later. They cannot sit upon Mother forever."

# XII

# ONE COOL CUSTOMER

ALTHOUGH Ramose was hopeful about speaking with his mother, unbelievable as it seemed, all afternoon somebody always seemed to be lounging upon her.

"She's got a pretty magnetic personality," Gerald remarked. "Even when she's quiet."

"What a great joke," Morgan laughed. "She's right under their noses."

"Amusing—until somebody lifts that sail and discovers her," replied Ramose, thoroughly worried.

While Ramose waited anxiously for a family reunion, the boys taught him the fundamentals of Ping-Pong. After all, he had made a pact: He would attempt to be their champ if they would assist him in finding his mother.

It was a real sacrifice, but to train their contender, the boys went to the game room at dawn. Miss Brickface was so pleased to see them up early for exercise, she pretty much left them alone. (Also, she was thrilled to help Dr. Smythe in grilling passengers regarding the stolen mummy. It was an excellent opportunity to get to know him—and to show off her range of hats.)

"He's a fascinating man," she confided once to the boys. "An expert on antiquities."

"Yeah," Gerald whispered under his breath. "So expert he thinks Ramose is just an average kid, plastered with graffiti."

When the boys showed Ramose the Ping-Pong equipment, he smiled. He liked the look of the Ping-Pong ball: small, white, and perfectly round. It fit in his hand like the turtle eggs he had once found beside the Great River—except the turtle eggs were rubbery.

Homesick and heartsick, while practicing the game, Ramose thought about the lush marshes along the Great River. He imagined the myriad plants growing there, the water lilies and papyrus and reeds and rushes. He thought of the waterfowl that inhabited the weeds, the geese and ibis and herons and ducks.

Ramose enjoyed whacking the Ping-Pong ball. Slamming it as hard as possible helped him vent his frustration over his family situation. In no time, he became ferociously good at the game.

The boys were ferociously pleased.

"You're a natural!" cried Morgan.

"You're born to win!" hollered Brandon.

Quincy yelled, "Look out, Pig Party, here comes Ramose!"

Ramose was not so confident. He worried almost constantly. *What if I let the boys down?* he wondered.

The search for the coffin was in full swing. The proper authorities had been notified in New York, and the ship would be met there by local police and searched yet again. Passengers were notified that at that time they might even be body searched.

"On your bod!" Gerald remarked sarcastically. "Great place to hide a coffin!"

The Ping-Pong tournament was also in full swing. Day by day, matches were completed. Day by day, contenders fell, hopefuls rose, until just two remained—Freddy Pig Party and Ramose.

The finals were to take place at noon. Ramose could win! The boys were excited out of their skulls.

As he entered the game room, Ramose gaped at the spectators jolting and jostling and jiggling and joggling to get a good view. It was as if every single person on board were there! He hated the idea of all those people oogling him—as if he were on display. His insides began throbbing like a drum.

He wanted to run away. But all he could think of was the boys—and his mother. He promised on the spot: *Mother, I will go to you the moment this contest is over.*

Ramose asked the boys anxiously, "What if I do not win?"

"No sweat. You're really gonna *cream* Freddy."

Ramose was unconvinced, but to the boys, he remarked as calmly as possible, "No sweatings. I am one cool customer."

Freddy Pig Party was waiting at the Ping-Pong table when the boys came in. At the first practice session, Gerald had unwrapped Ramose's stiff hands like the finest surgeon on the face of the map. The boys had all oohed and aahed at his most cool gold fingernail caps—and at his amazing state of shriveledness. Then Gerald had carefully re-wrapped them in modern bandages with plenty of flex, so Ramose could grasp a Ping-Pong paddle.

"Hello," Ramose said shyly to his opponent.

"Hey, freakshow!"

Then the match was on.

Freddy Pig Party's jaw locked in a smirky smile. His eyes bored into Ramose. He swatted the ball with crushing strokes, once actually popping it. Luckily, there were lots of back-ups.

Both players had cheering sections. Both loudly urged them on.

"Kill that ball!"

"Wham it!"

"Blam it!"

"Ram it down his throat!"

There was so much racket, Ramose had no idea if the catcalls were for Freddy or for him.

*Pock! Pock! Thock! Thock!* The Ping-Pong ball scorched back and forth over the net. The players were pretty well matched, so the score was even.

A referee kept yelling out the score. "Nine to nine!" "Twelve to twelve!" "Sixteen to sixteen!"

Freddy Pig Party acted like a real hotshot. The whole time he sizzled insults at Ramose:

"You're a klutz and a half!"

"You're a whiner!"

"You can't hit the side of an ocean liner!"

"You play like your *mother*!"

Freddy's other remarks had left Ramose unfazed. But he took the last jibe as a personal affront. It sent him into a Ping-Pong "zone." From then on, Ramose could do no wrong. It was razzle-dazzle all the way! What astounding shots! Underspin, overspin, topspin, bottomspin, reverse side-underspin—whatever spin was known, Ramose spun it at Freddy.

Again and again he sent the little white missile whizzing across the table. He moved like a cheetah, highly agile for a boy who had not moved much in the last four-thousand-plus years. Under his whacking style, Freddy Pig Party crumbled. Even Ramose was astounded at that.

The score was twenty to sixteen. One more point for the ship championship.

Dr. Smythe and Miss Brickface—sporting a flamingo-colored floppy hat—were watching the Ping-Pong match.

"Who *is* he?" Dr. Smythe asked.

"A student at Pharaoh's Academy," replied Miss Brickface. "Obviously he's not one of *our* boys."

"Bosh!" cried Dr. Smythe. Since meeting him, Dr. Smythe had been trying to unravel the mystery of Ramose's identity. His puckered face. His peculiar clothes. Dr. Smythe was certain that he knew Ramose.

*"Hold everything! Suspend play!"* Dr. Smythe suddenly bellowed from the sidelines. *"That player is a mummy!"*

"Cheat!" Freddy Pig Party shouted. "You're *way* over the age limit! You're no kid, you're a crummy old mummy!"

The spectators were baffled.

"What's the matter?"

"Who *is* he—an escaped convict?"

"He's a mummy, dummy!"

Ramose did not wait to discuss the issue. He ran.

*Ha-hoooga! Ha-hoooga! Ha-hoooga!* The ship's horns blared.

From watching the match, the kids especially were crazy about Ramose. He had a friendly personality, a shy but sparkling smile, and he displayed good sportsmanship. They did not much like Freddy, or the excitable man who had broken things up. So, many young people "accidentally" stuck out their feet to stop anybody from catching Ramose.

"*Oopsaleena!*" cried a girl in a pink tank top and everything to match (including her hair), sending Dr. Smythe sprawling and sputtering.

"*Oopsaleena!*" Other kids gaily took up the cry, doing their utmost to block the pursuers.

When Ramose fled, Gerald and the other boys scrammed, too. They had not been selected to go on a field trip to Egypt for nothing. They had brains in abundance.

"Quick!" yelled Gerald, on the run. "Disguise him!"

Before you could say "Nefertiti's nightgown," Ramose was lounging in a deck chair, swaddled in a first-class towel, swigging lemonade, complete with a tiny pink umbrella and a wedge of pink grapefruit.

"I regret that I failed you," Ramose told the boys sadly.

"*Fail!* You were *winning!*" shouted Gerald.

"Well, I regret that I am complicating your lives."

"It's the most fun *I've* had since my iguana got loose in the market!" said Quincy.

"But I regret—"

"You're gonna regret getting caught," Gerald whispered. "We gotta get outta here—to throw Smythe off your trail."

Ramose sat in the deck chair, thinking. Somewhere on the ship strangers were trying to capture him. Somewhere on the ship his mother was stuffed into a lifeboat. Somewhere on the ship Freddy Pig Party was probably gloating about winning—a hollow victory, really, since his opponent had been forced to flee for his life.

Ramose thought, *I was once a prince living in a palace, wearing marvelous clothing. I had a loving family. Now I am sitting in a stiff chair, swathed in a towel, all by myself.*

Ramose had no idea what to do. Things had grown terribly complicated. Somehow he had to save himself in order to save his mother. At the moment, he could not even go *near* her. Would he ever gaze upon her dear face again?

"Father, what should I do?" he said, looking up.

That is when Ramose felt the first raindrops.

# XIII

# MUMMY OVERBOARD!

AT first Ramose enjoyed the feel of the cooling raindrops upon his face. But in a matter of moments,
what had begun as a scattered shower became a
squall, then a storm, then a full-blown tempest.
Enormous amounts of water sloshed down from
the sky, as if dumped from colossal urns. Where had
so much water come from? It poured down in such
vast quantities and was frothed so wildly by wind,
it was soon hard to tell which was sea and which
was sky.

Everywhere above, black clouds boiled and roiled, as if they were furious. Lightning sliced through them constantly, adding its own frenzy to the scene.

At home, Ramose had experienced many sandstorms in which mad winds lifted the surface of the desert and sent it lashing everything in sight with stinging grit, pitting palaces and obelisks and sphinxes. Even now he could almost taste the dust, feel the whip of the sand's glassy grains against his bare legs. But in all his life, he had never experienced a storm like this.

Ramose felt miserable. His towel was soggy. The little pink umbrella was sodden. He was drenched to the very core.

Still, he was confident that in such weather, the search for him would be called off. So, though heavy with water, Ramose carefully arose (still gripping the lemonade glass, a thin disguise, just in case) and gazed over the ship's rail. What had been placid waves were by now huge rollers, smooth and dark as if gouged from polished black marble. Like a gull, tempest-tossed, the ship pitched in and out of the waves' fearful troughs.

Pretty soon, Ramose was not alone. Clearly the violence of the storm had sent swarms of people topside. Unfortunately, most of them were clinging to the rail, heaving into the heaving sea, both passengers and crew.

But Ramose did not feel the slightest bit bilious. Perhaps because he was accustomed to sailing up the Great River. Perhaps because he was a mummy without any innards. Who understands, truly, the workings of the body?

Amongst the throng of seasick people, Ramose spotted the boys. They seemed to be as ill, if not more so, than anybody. He longed to rush to their aid. To comfort them. To say, "Dear friends, do not be queasy." But he did not dare. It was best to remain under the dripping towel, alone.

Suddenly, thoughts of his mother flooded his mind. Was she safe? He looked at the lifeboat, where she was ensconced. In such a fearful storm, the sight of it was his only comfort.

Ramose gripped the railing, worrying. At any moment the ship could be swallowed by the sea. Then where would they be?

Without warning, the ship tilted. The coffin popped free of the lifeboat and landed on the deck with a terrific *smack*! Even though they were seasick, Ramose saw all the people swivel their heads toward the sound. For a moment, everything froze. The entire ship gazed, amazed, at the rain-glazed mummy case and the golden mask of his mother's face!

Dr. Smythe was in the crowd.

"There she is!" he yelled.

There she *was.* Just then the ship pitched again, sending the ponderous coffin skittering across the rain-soaked deck and crashing into the rail. With a crack like doom, the rail bent! The glittering casket teetered over the lip of the ship and tottered above the surging sea!

Dr. Smythe shouted into the wind, "Mummy overboard!"

*Ha-hoooga! Ha-hoooga! Ha-hoooga!* Alarms gasped and coughed.

"*Mother!*" Ramose screamed. Then he swooned.

# XIV

# COLD TRAIL

THE next day dawned clear, as though no cloud had ever formed before or ever even *thought* about raining. Above the sea arched the great expanse of sky, as blue as faience. The only reminders of the storm were little shivers of water that clung to the rail ringing the ocean liner.

With great effort, Ramose slogged out from behind a large equipment box. When he had come to his senses after collapsing, he had crouched there, in hiding. Dazed with grief, he stared ahead, seeing nothing.

"Mother, I have let you down miserably," he moaned into the briny wind. "Now you are gone forever."

He felt unbearably sad.

"Ramose," somebody whispered. "You OK?"

It was Gerald.

"All is lost. Mother is drowned. She is food for fishes," he mourned. "I am the one remaining—and good-for-nothing—member of our family line."

"You're wrong," Gerald said in a kind way. "She's fine."

Ramose was stunned beyond belief. Hope surged throughout his being. *"What do you mean?"* he screamed.

"Dr. Smythe recaptured her and carted her off."

Ramose went limp, weak with relief. Silently, he thanked every god he knew.

"How can it be?" he asked. "Give me all the details—please!"

"How did you miss it?"

"I think I fainted."

"Jeez! No wonder you're so bummed out." Gerald spoke sympathetically. As fast as possible, he related the events.

"When the coffin rammed the rail, it got pretty well wedged," Gerald said. "Dr. Smythe and a bunch of guys prised it loose with crowbars, pummeled the whole time by raindrops the size of dates. It was great to see them soaked to the gills."

As a boy, Ramose had loved dates. Upon hearing this description, he loved them more.

"I am sorry I missed that," remarked Ramose. Then he eagerly asked, "Where is Mother now?"

"Probably with Dr. Smythe's luggage."

"I must go to her."

"No *way*. Look. The trip's over."

Gerald pointed out to sea. Ramose looked up. Before them rose a stunning sight—monument after monument, so tall, so grand, so shining! For what mighty pharaohs had they had been built? Ramose could not possibly imagine. The most magnificent of these was a statue of a woman hefting a torch.

Ramose gaped, struck dumb.

"That's Manhattan Island, New York City," Gerald explained. "Where they're taking your mother." Then he told Ramose, "I gotta go. The boys and me, we're sorta, kinda in a little trouble."

"What is the problem?"

"Somebody finally noticed my briefcase—outside the green door. They figure we're in cahoots."

"Ca-*whats*?"

"That we're in it together—and that we're the mummy snatchers."

"Oh, my goodness!" cried Ramose, very worried indeed. "Will there be loppings of heads?"

Head loppings had never occurred to Gerald.

"We'll be OK. We'll say we used the place for studying. Studying makes grown-ups delirious with joy."

Ramose was relieved, for he knew that was true.

"You can grab a cab to get where you're going," said Gerald. "The shipping line's providing them free for everybody—because of the storm, 'for the inconvenience,' they said."

Actually, the shipping company had no control over the weather. Still, it was a nice gesture.

"What is a cab?"

"A taxi. A machine with wheels. You'll see. Well, good-bye."

"Farewell?" asked Ramose awkwardly.

"Yep," said Gerald. "Sorry we weren't much help with your mother."

"I am sorry I did not crush your Freddy."

Just then the other boys rushed up.

"Gotta go, Gerald. Here comes Miss B. We're off to the Inquisition."

"The what?"

"To answer five zillion questions."

In a splurge of emotion, Hunter took off his baseball cap and put it on Ramose. Backwards. "Root for the Yankees." He stuck a thumb up.

Ramose touched the beautiful baseball cap. A lump filled his throat. He whispered, "I shall never remove it."

"Good-bye! Good-bye! Good-bye!" The boys waved to Ramose.

Gerald yelled, "Good luck, friend! And watch it! Dr. Smythe's still looking for you."

"Do not concern yourself. I am one cool customer."

Waving as gaily as possible, Ramose watched the boys depart. In his new cap, he knew that he looked cool, like a swiveled-around duck. He smiled weakly—sad, but also happy.

Wistfully, he said aloud, "I am a friend to boys."

Already he missed them. He felt as if a small hole had opened somewhere inside him.

The boys were gone. Miss Brickface was gone. Dr. Smythe and Ramose's mother were gone. Ramose had seen people lugging her coffin off the ship. Helpless, he had watched her go. He was just a boy. There was nothing he could do.

Suddenly a horrifying thought nearly knocked him over—he had forgotten where Dr. Smythe was taking his mother!

# XV

# HOMELESS

RAMOSE stood bewildered at the dock. Except for journeys with his father to the Land of Punt, seeking frankincense, he had never risked going far from home. Nothing was in the least familiar in this strange land. Not a pyramid, not a palm, not a grain of sand. The throb of activity around him was so unsettling he wanted to hide. Ramose felt as though all of his senses had funneled out of him, like grain emptied from a sack.

A bright yellow taxi pulled up.

"Say," remarked the driver, glimpsing Ramose, "that storm musta been a pip! You look like a dog's breakfast!" Then he added, "Where to?"

"I do not know," Ramose replied, forlorn.

"I ain't got all day," the cabby growled. "The boat line paid me to take you anyplace in Manhattan. Gimme a destination."

"Uh . . . uh . . . ," Ramose stammered. Then, with home on his mind, he blurted, "New Stork City."

"That's New *York*, buddy. And you're there already."

"I *am*?"

"Hey, are you for real?" snapped the cabby.

"Yes, indeed," declared Ramose timidly. "Truly, I forget where I wish to go."

"OK," replied the cabby, "we play it this way. I take you to a favorite location o' mine and drop you there. How's that sound?"

"That sounds very nice," said Ramose "—except the dropping off part. I am a quite fragile personage."

"For Pete's sakes, hop in," grumbled the cabby.

As soon as he did, the taxi lurched off. The trip was exhilarating. Very rough. Very jolty. Very wild. It was not at all like being borne on his father's palanquin. Ramose loved going fast. He was sorry when they reached the end of the trip.

"This is it," said the cabby. "Central Park. Enjoy."

Curious, but afraid to offend, Ramose asked timidly, "What is a park?"

"For the love o' Mike!" the cabby shouted and took off.

Ramose looked around. As in the port where his sea journey had begun, cars roared up and down a great tar path, a "street," as the old woman who had helped him called it. Oh, the smells! Oh, the activity! Oh, the cacophony of horns! Oh, the smack of small boards with wheels, *dit-dit-dit*-ing over cracks! He felt light-headed. There were monuments, monuments, monuments. People, people, people. They swarmed everywhere, like ants on the move, speaking their many tongues, going their many ways. Their raiments were quite marvelous—especially compared with his rags.

On one side of the street, the monuments spired into the sky, staring with innumerable shining and frightening eyes. Across the street was a large field full of white patches and strange leafless trees. The grooves of their bark were dusted with white. A most marvelous sight, indeed.

"How sad. The trees are dead," Ramose whispered to himself. He wondered what plague had struck them down.

Amazed though he was by the sights, Ramose could think only of those he loved. The boys. He missed their cheerfulness. Their jokes. He hoped they were, as they said, "OK." And the comfort of his mother's nearness. Where was she? If only he knew the name of the place where she was going. Being so far from her was nearly too much to bear.

*"Remember! Remember!"* he urged himself. But the more he thought, the more he forgot. Ramose doubted his capabilities more than ever. No boy was up to such a task, especially one who had done nothing on his own. He had no hope of finding her. Ramose wished simply to lie down and die. But, of course, he would fail at that, too—he was already dead.

As if in a world woven of crazy dreams, Ramose stumbled along, shivering from the cold. His teeth were chattering so much, he hoped he would not chatter them right out of his skull. He hoped to wake up laughing soon, close to his mother in the tomb. Slowly, he entered the place of the field and slumped down upon a long seat.

"Where you from?" asked the man slumped next to him.

In his grief, Ramose had not noticed him before.

The man wore tattered garments as grimy as his own, and hand-coverings that looked as if a jackal had chewed them. They resembled each other in many ways, except that the man was older and had foot-coverings with large tongues hanging out of them, as if they were panting.

"I come from the land of sand."

"Palm Springs?"

Upon hearing the name of his favorite tree, Ramose perked up a little.

"I guess so," he replied as truthfully as possible. At home, there were both palms and springs.

"So you've struck bottom, my friend," guessed the man. "Like me."

Since the man took him for a boy with no home, Ramose decided against raising the mummy issue.

"I am far below bottom," replied Ramose sadly. "I

have lost my home. I have nowhere to go. Worst of all, I have lost my mother."

"I once had a mother. . . ." mused the man in reverie.

All was quiet for a time. Perhaps he was reflecting upon some sweet memory of home.

"My place isn't much, but you can stay with me."

"Something is better than nothing," replied Ramose gratefully.

The two stood up and began shuffling along a narrow path. As they went, they conversed.

"What is the great, cold whiteness everywhere upon the ground?" Ramose asked meekly, for he was certain that even the dogs that passed knew quite well what it was.

"Snow," replied the homeless man. "None o' that out in Palm Springs?"

"Not that I have seen. What is it exactly?"

"Water, from the sky. Frozen." The man shivered as he spoke. "It's cold, but it hides man's mistakes."

"Like what?"

"Like garbage."

"Who freezes it?" asked Ramose.

"Who knows?"

They reached the place where the man lived, deep in a snowy pile of brush. The man glanced over his shoulder—once, twice—then burrowed inside.

"Come in—and welcome."

The brush pile was hollowed in the center and filled with many objects, most of which Ramose did not recognize. They turned out to be things called bottles and soda-pop cans and Ziploc bags and paper cups and hubcaps and footwear with spikes and boxer shorts with designs of ants. There was a dented saucepan, a pink eraser, and a lovely orange construction cone. One lumpish slab was a mattress, for sleeping.

"Home sweet home," said the man.

"This is very nice, indeed," Ramose said, though the brush pile was nothing like his father's palace.

He was especially inquisitive about the items that looked like scrolls of papyrus. Back home, scribes took a long time preparing these. Nobody else knew how. Some were lists of personal holdings. Others were letters about this and that. All were highly prized.

"What are these?" Ramose asked.

"Newspapers," replied the man.

"*The New York Times*? That is what Gerald and the other boys read."

"Yep," grunted the man. "'All the News That's Fit to Print.'"

"Perhaps these pages hold news of my mother," Ramose whispered.

"Maybe," said the man. "But they're pretty old."

"Do you think other scrolls will have news of her? She really is quite famous."

"Might. Tomorrow we'll scrounge some up and see."

But that was not to be. Without warning, somebody outside shouted. "Come outta there! No loitering in the park!"

"The cops!" cried the man. "They're tossin' me out again! Quick—hide under the mattress!"

# XVI

# FRIENDS IN
# LOW PLACES

WEEKS passed. Sometimes snow blew itself over the park; sometimes it held its breath. Ramose's new acquaintance did not return. He had been hustled off from his brush-pile home by something called "cops"—before Ramose could give him thanks for his kindness.

During that time, Ramose wandered aimlessly along the paths of the park. He never strayed too far; the city was overwhelming. It was still winter, but he had gotten a little used to the cold. Even so, he plucked *The New York Times* from a trash bin and wrapped it around his shoulders for warmth. Or he wrapped his own arms around himself. All the time he thought of his mother. Where was she? He could not remember.

It was daybreak. The first sip of sun kissed the horizon. The earth was still, except for some small rustlings near Ramose's head. Alone and forlorn, he felt too unhappy to move. But he was very curious about the noises close by, so at last he opened his eyes.

"Hey, kiddo," said a voice near his ear. "Nice digs."

"Digs?"

"Living quarters."

Quivering beneath the mattress where he lay sleepless, Ramose asked, "Who are you? Cops?"

Ramose peeked out, sideways, and saw a bird, gray and beautiful, with lovely pink feet the color of the eraser he had seen, and a neck with the sheen of a rainbow. With his thick beak, the bird poked everything in sight, constantly bobbing his head. Ramose was delighted to see a fowl similar to those of his homeland.

"I'm just a pigeon, lookin' fer a smidgen o' somethin'. Tryin' to survive. Ya know how it is. Name's Vinny," the pigeon said.

Ramose marveled at how he could understand animals. First a camel, then a snake, now a bird. What a mysterious and wondrous world!

"I am Ramose," said Ramose. "I do not know pigeons. Just turtledoves. I am pleased to meet you."

"Ditto, kiddo."

"This digs is not mine," Ramose explained. "It belongs to a man, tossed out—into the snow. It is a sad place, I think, where a man cannot have even a brush pile of his own."

"I couldn't agree more," replied Vinny.

"I am like the man of this place," said Ramose.

"Homeless?" inquired Vinny.

"Yes. If I were pharaoh, I would give everybody a home."

"You can never go wrong on the side of kindness," remarked Vinny. "Hey, what's this *phay-roe* stuff?"

"I am Ramose, a mummy," Ramose explained for the thousandth time.

"Always hoped ta know one o' them," replied the pigeon.

"So you believe me?"

"Hey, I've heard it all. No tale's too fantastic. Let's take a stroll while you fill me in on the details of your life."

They left the hideout where they had been chatting and ambled down the street, beneath the canopy of brown trees.

"Why are the trees dead, Vinny?" asked Ramose.

"They're not. Soon things'll be on the upswing. Life'll renew, ya know?"

"You mean the trees will arrive at the Afterlife?"

"In a manner of speaking. They'll get a fresh start."

To hear Ramose better, Vinny perched on his shoulder, head bobbing, eyes bright. As they walked, Ramose related his tale—of grave robbers, camels, snakes, bedouins, museum representatives, and other scary things. His small and worried voice droned on and on, interrupted now and then by Vinny's remarks:

"Is that a fact?"

"Ya don't say!"

"Jeez, Louise!"

"Grave robbers—every mother's dream!"

When Ramose finished, Vinny shouted, "Stole yer mother! That's *criminal*! You're in a real pickle!"

"What is a pickle?" asked Ramose, very worried indeed.

"A small vegetable," Vinny explained.

"I am in a small vegetable?" Ramose looked at himself, puzzled.

"Merely an expression. Means ya got problems."

Ramose already knew that. "Will you help me?" he asked desperately.

"Certainly," replied Vinny with vigor. "Those guys of which you speak gotta lotta nerve, waltzing off with somebody's mother. Mothers are sacred. It ain't every day one gets the opportunity to defend one's moral principles, kiddo. Deal me in."

"Does that mean yes?" Ramose asked hopefully.

"Most certainly does! Now first off, we gotta devise a plan. Second off, where's yer mother, the queen?"

Suddenly, a memory zinged him from nowhere.

"*Now I remember!*" yelled Ramose, highly agitated. "*She is in the museum!*"

"I hate to be the bearer of bad news," Vinny began, "but in this town, museums are a dime a dozen. To which one are you referrin'?"

Ramose plunged into gloom darker than the vulture-wing black of his tomb.

"I forget," he said miserably.

"Hey, kiddo, do not be dismal," Vinny exhorted. "I enjoy art. I know all the museums. We'll figger it out. Just gimme a minute."

Vinny fluttered down from Ramose's shoulder.

"I do my best thinkin' wid my feet on *terra firma*," he stated, "if ya know what I mean."

"I do not," said Ramose truthfully.

"I think best wid my feet upon the ground," Vinny explained. "Speakin' o' the ground, there's a nice tidbit." Vinny gobbled a chunk of something from the sidewalk. "Can't beat a bagel," he remarked. "Now then, let's talk museums. Could be the Frick," Vinny mused aloud to himself. "Nope. Too old-world. Guggenheim? Pretty modern for a mummy. Museum of the American Indian? I don't think so, Vinny. She's Egyptian. That one's too—uh—American Indian. How 'bout that little gem over on—nah," he interrupted himself. "Atmosphere ain't quite right."

While Vinny was working things out, Ramose wiggled a lot.

"Stop fidgettin', kiddo. You're throwin' me off," Vinny said. "Compose yerself. Stand still. Like me."

Ramose stood as still as he possibly could under the circumstances. Once, quickly, he glanced at Vinny. He noticed Vinny's feet. He noticed his own.

"Look, Vinny!" he cried with delight. "We are standing in exactly the same way!"

"Restrain yourself, I'm thinkin'," said Vinny, but he took a look at his own feet.

"That's pigeon-toed, kiddo. My natural stance."

"But I am also pigeon-toed!" shouted Ramose, very excited. "Do you think we could perhaps, be—brothers?"

Vinny glanced at Ramose's feet. Bundled though they were, they pointed inward.

"It's a stretch," he replied, a little surprised, "but hold on to the thought."

Ramose clutched the thought very tightly, indeed. At this time, when the boys and his mother were lost to him, he desperately needed a blood relation—somebody who had good ideas, somebody who could remember things, somebody upon whom he could rely.

In his excitement over this possible family connection, Ramose blundered into the street.

*Va-roooom!* At the same moment, belching fumes, a metro bus roared up.

"Help!" yelled Ramose.

# XVII

## THE TRAIL HEATS UP

THE metro bus swooshed by, nearly squashing Ramose. He got a good dusting, but jumped back onto the sidewalk in the nick of time.

"Jeez, kiddo, you OK?" asked Vinny, his voice thick with concern.

"I th-th-think so," stammered Ramose, trembling with fright.

"That bus nearly blew ya down," said Vinny. "No wonder. You're a real lightweight, due to yer evisceration."

"My e-*what*?"

"Evisceration—mummification. I read about it once in the *Times*. Years back, in your land, guys called embalmers—real professionals—eliminated the corpse of its vitals—lungs, intestines, liver, et cetera—an' dried it out, like a gigantic mushroom. Took a coupla months. Mine's a real simplified explanation, but, basically, the body was all set for the Afterlife. Real fascinatin' stuff."

Vinny spoke with great enthusiasm, his head wig-wagging all the while.

"Vinny, could you discuss something else?" asked Ramose timidly. He did not wish to offend his new friend, but this conversation made him squeamish.

"Jeez, forgive my churlishness! My total lack o' sensitivity!" Vinny said, apologizing profusely. "One minute, yer nearly mashed; the next, some bozo's discussin' yer innards. What was I *thinkin'*?"

"It is, as you say, OK," replied Ramose. "I always knew about mummies. It is just that now the subject is, well, personal."

"Sure," said Vinny. "Hey, let's sit down, so's ya can gather yourself."

Vinny hopped onto the armrest of a bench.

Ramose was about to join him on the bench, but he stopped midway and shouted, "Vinny! The side of the bus! It displayed a likeness of Mother!"

"Kiddo, that's *great!*" yelled Vinny, fluttering up. "Good detective work!"

"Defective?"

"*Detective*. Ya figured it out."

"What does it matter?" asked Ramose sadly. "The bus is gone. We will never find it."

"No problem," chirped Vinny.

Suddenly, he plowed his feathers with his beak, then nibbled something vigorously.

"What are you *doing*, Vinny?" asked Ramose, terribly anxious to know what Vinny was about to say.

"Killin' mites—little bugs—they're real pests."

"Please," Ramose pleaded, "tell me why there is no bus problem."

"Oh, yeah," said Vinny. "Lost my train o' thought. As I was sayin', when there's an art exhibit in this city, *all* the buses are plastered with posters. Actually, everything's pretty bannered-up with related info. I was too busy thinkin' to think—if ya know what I mean. Look, kiddo. That yer mother?"

Vinny raised a wing in the direction of a banner

fluttering from a lamppost. (In fact, nearly every lamppost proclaimed the news.)

"Oh, Vinny!" cried Ramose, overjoyed. "It is she!"

He gazed at the face upon the banner lovingly, unable to focus upon anything else.

Vinny read the banner aloud with all the drama he could muster: "The Ancient Majesty of Queen Neferet. The Central Museum of Art. Permanent collection."

"What a ninny, Vinny," Vinny chastised himself. "How couldya forget the Central? Why didn't ya at least look up? The whole time she was right under yer beak." To Ramose he said, "We got the dope, thanks to you, kiddo. We know the location of yer mother."

"Where?" asked Ramose eagerly.

"The Central. Right down the street."

"The Central. That is the museum of which my friend Gerald spoke," said Ramose.

"Excellent. Banners are fine," said Vinny, "but it's best to get personal confirmation. Now, the good news is, yer mother's in the permanent collection. That means, she ain't goin' nowhere. The bad news is—"

He might as well have been talking to himself. For suddenly, Ramose turned and clumped off.

"Hey, kiddo! Where ya goin'?" Vinny shouted.

Ramose hustled down the street. The melting snow slurped at his feet.

New Yorkers love to run, so there were many other joggers about. But Ramose was the only one who was bandaged and graffitied from head to foot. Ignoring Vinny's shouts, he stumped clumsily but quickly along the sidewalk, in the direction of the Central Museum of Art.

# XVIII

# THE CURSE OF THE RABID MUMMY

RAMOSE was moving as fast as he possibly could, considering that he was so heavily bound.

"Mother, I am nearly there!"

As he went, he repeated this in his head, like a prayer, hoping that the thoughts would reach her. That wherever she was in the place called the Central, she would hear him and take heart.

He had to be careful not to bump into people—out of courtesy, of course, but also because he was fragile. One good thump would mean certain disintegration.

"*Whaddaya think yer doin'? Stop!*" Vinny suddenly swooped up and alighted on Ramose's head.

Ramose kept going.

"I am going to rescue my mother," he explained.

"Kiddo, one does not just go bustin' inta the Central. One's gotta devise a *plan.*"

"But *why?*" asked Ramose impatiently.

"First off, yer mother's the main attraction, the 'piece of resistance,' as they say. She'll be under heavy guard," explained Vinny. "You'll get caught. Second off, ditto. Get my drift, kiddo?"

"I will get caught?" asked Ramose, slowing down.

"Precisely."

"That would not be so bad, Vinny," said Ramose. "Then Mother and I would be together."

"Correct me if I'm wrong, but I thought the two of you had to get back to yer tomb. To complete that Great Journey you've been waitin' for forever."

"You are right," said Ramose, embarrassed by his own foolishness. At last he stopped. "Upon seeing Mother's face, all other thoughts rushed away. Oh, Vinny, it is so difficult being a boy."

"Why is that?"

"Because I think like a boy. I am not clever. I wish I could think like my father."

"Ya think just fine, kiddo," said Vinny. "Ya got a good noggin."

"Noggin?"

"Head. Actually, I'm referrin' to yer brain."

"Thank you, Vinny," said Ramose shyly. "I hate to remind myself of such matters, but I believe my brain is gone."

"Oh, yeah," remarked Vinny, "but ya got yerself this far, so *somethin's* workin'."

"It has all been pure luck. Please, Vinny," Ramose pleaded, "will you help me to devise a plan? I do not think that I can."

"Sure, kiddo."

"What is the plan?" Ramose asked anxiously.

"Not so fast. Plans do not just *poof* to life by magic. We gotta ponder a bit. Organize. Let the ideas gel."

"While we are thinking," said Ramose, "could we visit Mother?"

"Consider it done."

But it wasn't. It was Monday, so the Central Museum was closed.

"I cannot stand it, Vinny," said Ramose. "Mother is just inside those doors, and yet I cannot see her!"

"Must be real nerve-rackin'," said Vinny sympathetically. "Keep yer chin up. Tomorrow we'll come back an' and case the joint. Size the place up—so's we know how best to spring yer mother."

"Spring?"

"Liberate. Set her free. Look," said Vinny, "ya gotta get yer mind off yer mother. Yer makin' yerself sick. Hey, I know just the ticket—a movie!"

"What is that?" asked Ramose.

"Wait an' see."

Directed by Vinny, who was perched upon his shoulder, Ramose crossed the park and headed for Broadway.

"Here we are," said Vinny, after their long ramble. "I thought you'd like this particular film, *The Curse of the Rabid Mummy*. Might make you feel at home."

The theater that Vinny had chosen looked a little shoddy. And it was pretty deserted. There were no customers in the ticket line.

"Lemme see, how are we gonna get in?" Vinny asked himself. "The money angle slipped my mind."

"What is money?" asked Ramose.

"Stuff with which to purchase things. Filthy lucre," explained Vinny.

"Could we barter?" suggested Ramose. "That is the custom at home."

"Whatcha got to trade?"

While Ramose and Vinny were discussing their finances, quite a crowd had gathered around Ramose. Perhaps the movie marquee had attracted their attention. Perhaps it was Ramose's wrappings. In any case, for once, people made the connection. They all gaped at him.

"What a great-looking mummy!" shouted a man.

"Hey! Walk like an Egyptian!" joked his companion.

"He looks so *real*!" shrieked a lady.

"Must be a real scary movie!" hollered a boy.

"I love to be scared," cried a girl. "Let's go in!"

Once the crowd was inside, the theater manager rushed to Ramose.

"Thanks, buddy!" he said enthusiastically. "Great promotional scheme! How can I repay you?"

"Let me see the movie?" Ramose suggested shyly, flustered by the attention.

"Be my guest," said the manager, bowing toward the entrance.

"May I bring a friend?" asked Ramose politely, not wishing to request too much.

"Who?" asked the manager.

"This bird," said Ramose, pointing at Vinny.

"Why not?" replied the manager. "He might enjoy it."

"Good thinkin', kiddo! Ya never cease to amaze me!" remarked Vinny as they entered the theater.

Actually, Ramose had surprised himself as well. The words had just popped into his head.

At the movies, people spilled food everywhere, Raisinets and popcorn and Jujubes. As soon as they were seated, Vinny hopped down and picked up something in his beak.

"Hot dog," he mumbled to Ramose, pecking at the morsel greedily.

Ramose brightened up.

"Where I come from, *all* dogs are hot," he remarked. "All people are hot. Mine is a very hot land."

"This ain't a real dog, kiddo."

"I am glad," Ramose said.

The movie was over. Ramose was stunned by what he had witnessed—a multitude of colorful images flashing before him upon a screen. He was even more stunned by their content, the story of a rabies-crazed mummy who raged through a city, clapping wrathful curses upon people and causing their deaths in a series of ghastly ways.

"Vinny, mummies do not put curses upon people!" cried Ramose. "Mummies do not curse anything! They just rest a lot!"

"I know, kiddo," Vinny agreed. "Somehow mummies've gotten a real bum rap."

"But *why*?"

"Beats me," responded Vinny. "Most people do not know a mummy on a personal basis, such as has been my privilege. If they did, they'd change their opinions."

"Does that mean that you—*like* me?" asked Ramose.

"Certainly," said Vinny.

Ramose was so pleased by Vinny's remarks, he coughed and adjusted his baseball cap. He also calmed down about the mummy's curse.

As Ramose and Vinny were leaving the theater, the manager hustled up to them.

"Can you come back tomorrow?" he asked eagerly.

"Tell 'im we got plans," said Vinny, steering Ramose back toward the park. He fluttered down now and then to sip melted snow from a gutter.

"Pretty quiet," said Vinny as they walked along. "What's on yer mind?"

"Mother. I cannot wait for tomorrow to come, to case the joint—and to see her!"

# XIX

## INSPIRATION

RAMOSE and Vinny returned to the park. As they neared their destination, Ramose looked up and saw a falcon perched in a tall plane tree.

"Vinny, look! In that tree!" he whispered hoarsely. "It is the great god, Horus!"

"Yer as innocent as a fresh-laid egg," snapped Vinny nervously. "That ain't no god, kiddo, that's Death."

"You are wrong," insisted Ramose. "Horus is the guardian of royalty. I take this as a strong sign that he is watching over us."

"He's watching us, all right—waiting to dive down and spear my gizzard for dinner. *I* take this as a strong sign that I'd better beat it!" cried Vinny, scuttling into the brush pile.

Reluctantly, Ramose followed him back inside the brush pile that had been abandoned by the homeless man. Luckily, no other police officers had come to roust them out. Ramose peered through the canopy of branches and soggy brown leaves, hoping to see Horus. Sure enough, the small falcon still perched high above, unmoving, like a small statue. Though Vinny seemed highly shaken by the raptor, its presence made Ramose's heart feel light.

It was twilight. The air grew thick and chilly. Little scarves of fog began misting through the brush, each wisp like a small gray mystery.

Ramose longed to figure out how to free his mother. Secretly, he wished that Gerald and the rest of the boys were with him now. He knew that they had magnificent brains—and that they were quite familiar with the museums, especially the one called the Central.

*We practically live at the Central.* Ramose heard Gerald's words in his head.

But Ramose did not mention these thoughts to Vinny. Vinny was proud of his background in art, and of his ability to survive on the street. Vinny had been a true friend to him. Ramose would not hurt his feelings for anything.

"What are we going to do, Vinny?" Ramose asked eagerly.

"I'm not quite sure, to tell ya the truth," replied Vinny. "So far, my idea's pretty sketchy. Not fully hatched."

"But what *is* it?"

"Tomorrow, first thing, you slip inside the Central," Vinny explained.

"By *myself*?" shrieked Ramose. "But I want *you* with me! You *must* assist me!"

"No dice, kiddo. No birds allowed. Sorry."

"But what if I am captured, Vinny?"

"It's a risk you'll hafta take," replied Vinny. "Just get a good look at the setup, an', o' course, locate yer mother. Then we'll figger out our next move. At this time, I'm in a real quandary about what that might be."

"I have visited such a quandary!" cried Ramose, greatly pleased, forgetting for the moment his worries about tomorrow. "My father took me there—to select the stones for his tomb!"

Once, Ramose and his father had traveled by boat, up the Great River, to the cliff of stone. He closed his eyes and could still see the rowers, dipping their oars into the dark water. He could still hear the splash of each dripping stroke. He could still see the sails, like egret wings. He could still see the sands at sunrise, sands the color of honey. Thinking about that long-ago trip made Ramose deeply homesick.

"You're talkin' quarry," replied Vinny, interrupting his trance. "I mean quandary, which is to say that I'm perplexed."

It was quiet inside the brush pile for a while, while both Vinny and Ramose tried to think.

"I'm stumped for ideas," Vinny finally said. "Yer friendly assassin's janglin' my nerves."

"He is *not* an assassin, Vinny. He is a protector."

"Oh, *brother*!"

"I do not know much about planning," said Ramose timidly, "but may I make a suggestion?"

"Sure thing. This is a democracy. Everybody puts his two cents in."

"What do you mean, Vinny?"

"Everybody gets his say."

"You are not ruled by pharaohs?" asked Ramose, surprised by this news.

"Nope," replied Vinny. "Not the last time I looked. The people here tried a king briefly, but it wasn't a positive experience."

"Who rules this land?"

"Everybody."

"Even *birds*?"

"Nope," replied Vinny. "People aren't smart enough for that. Now, gettin' back to yer thought . . ."

"Father loved war," said Ramose. "Though I was a boy, he loved discussing it with me. He loved to make the enemy look the other way, then sweep in and capture him."

"A ruse! Of *course*!" shouted Vinny, fluttering up and spiraling around Ramose delightedly. "You create a diversion, then snatch your mother and vamoose!"

"My father was very good at war," said Ramose proudly. "He took many captives."

"*What a revoltin' thought!*" Vinny yelled.

Ramose was embarrassed. He stammered, "C-c-captives showed that a ruler was strong. Then his enemies left him alone."

"This is a sore subject with me," groused Vinny. "People keep birds in cages, ya know. A first-class abomination! Freedom is for every single living creature! That's the name o' that tune!"

"I never thought of it like that before," said Ramose sheepishly. "It was always our custom."

"I'm sure yer father was a fine person," grumbled Vinny. "Other times, other ways, I guess."

"Is my idea a good one?" Ramose asked.

"Kiddo, it's an *inspiration*!"

"How will we use this plan, Vinny?"

"Lemme sleep on it." With that, Vinny fell dead to the world.

Ramose was too overwrought to sleep. Tomorrow, if all went well, he would locate his mother. He lay upon his back, looking up. Outside, through the vagrant fog, the eyes of the monuments shone as though every star in the endless heavens had come down to cluster about them.

He hoped that Horus was still watching, outside in the dark.

"Great Feathered One," Ramose whispered to the falcon, "help Vinny and me, please, to devise a good plan—and please keep my mother from harm."

# XX

# CASING THE JOINT

IT was morning, gloomy with fog and chill. Winter had gone to somewhere else. Ramose smelled something new in the air. Something unsettling. Something that made him fidget. What *was* it?

He and Vinny were standing at the top of the steps outside of the Central Museum of Art, between two stone columns crowned with stone leaves—not the palm or papyrus or lotus he knew. Still, this pillared monument was not unlike the palace of a pharaoh. From either side of the building hung enormous purple banners announcing the special exhibit—

announcing its "piece of resistance," as Vinny had called it—Queen Neferet, Ramose's mother.

Because Ramose was overeager, they had arrived quite a while ago. Now they waited for the museum to open. Ramose paced up and down, frantic with anticipation.

"Compose yerself, kiddo," said Vinny, preening his feathers, "or you'll experience a nervous collapse."

"I cannot help it, Vinny," replied Ramose. "My excitement is too great. Soon, I fear, I shall explode into many small pieces."

"Don't," snapped Vinny. "Besides—it's open now. You can go in. I'll be here when you come out."

"But what do I *do*?"

"Blend in, kiddo. An' follow the crowd. They'll lead ya straight to yer mother."

The doors swung wide. Many people pressed in, anxious, no doubt, to view the ancient queen— the "Old Prune," as the grave robber had referred to her.

Frightened though he was, Ramose joined the throng.

He entered the great hall and gasped at its size and at the white marble floors, polished to a glare.

He looked straight before him, over the heads of the milling people. On either side of the hall stood a gigantic urn, blazing with flowers. For a moment he stood gazing, inhaling their sweet fragrance. He felt comforted in this room, for the urns and the flowers reminded him of home.

*Which way?* Ramose asked himself.

But before he could decide, a guard stepped up to him.

"Pardon me, young man," said the guard, "where's your button?"

"Button?" Ramose gaped.

"To prove you paid the entrance fee," she said.

"Oh, *that* button." Ramose's thoughts raced. "I—uh—lost it."

"I'm sorry," the guard said. "You cannot enter without a chartreuse button. Chartreuse is the color of the day."

"Oh," replied Ramose, deeply disappointed. Slowly, he walked back out.

"That was quick," remarked Vinny, gulping a hunk of doughnut someone had dropped. "How's yer mother?"

"I cannot see her," Ramose explained, utterly

beside himself. "A guard said I do not have the proper button."

"Don't let that stop ya," replied Vinny. "We'll find one. Did the official in question happen to mention what color?"

"Chartreuse."

"Disgusting," remarked Vinny. "You'd think they'd come up with a better shade, like, say—*gray*. I'll look for one. I'm closer to the ground than you."

Pretty soon Vinny scrounged up a chartreuse button. Ramose put it on, carefully bending the tab over the strip of his wrapping material. Ramose grinned. Imagine! This small green button would get him closer to his mother!

"Vinny?" he turned and asked earnestly.

"Yeah?"

"If you ever have a child, will you name it Chartreuse?"

Vinny gave him a friendly look.

"If I have a child, I shall name it Ramose." He coughed, embarrassed. "Now, go find your mother!"

Nervously, Ramose entered the Central again. This time, the guard let him pass. He followed the large and noisy crowd into the Egyptian section, his mouth open at the wonders—and the visitors. People pushed and shoved, apparently very eager to view his mother. Like a river of mud, the throng slowly nudged Ramose into a large room.

"Oh, my goodness!" he whispered.

All at once, he was engulfed with memories, as if he had stepped inside a great cluster of butterflies. In small cases everywhere around him were objects that he recognized! Despite the crowd, Ramose rushed from case to case joyfully. He wanted to laugh. He wanted to cry. He wanted to touch all the beloved things before him, but dared not.

Vinny had warned him, "Ya touch any museum stuff, ya get tossed."

What a marvelous array! Carved stones like those upon his father's tomb, showing armed troops running. And scenes in relief of his most-loved seasons, shemu, the harvest, and akhet, the green time of inundation. There was a carving of donkeys ankle-deep in grain. (Once, in a fit of kindness, Ramose had sneaked into the threshing room and released such poor beasts.) And figurines of people he once had known—the potter, the butcher, and the flour-dusted miller, hunched over her grinding stone.

Ramose could barely contain himself, he felt so close to his beloved land. Suddenly, he paused and looked up. On one wall hung a beaded shroud— the raiment of a queen.

"Oh, giddy son! How distracted I have become!" Ramose groaned. "Where is Mother?"

His mother, Queen Neferet, was easy to spot. A multitude ringed her coffin, craning their necks for a good view. The coffin lay open, but, covered by a slab of glass, she was unable to escape. Beneath it, her eyes, swiped with color, looked up from her pitch-dark face, as if horrified by all the commotion. Thanks to the grave robber who'd unwrapped her head to have a look-see, everybody could now do the same. The visitors oogled her from all angles, just as Morgan had said they would.

Trembling, Ramose made his way (carefully) close to the coffin. Oh, the dear and shriveled face! He remembered the greeting that he had practiced on the ship for this occasion.

"Mother, I am here." Ramose uttered the words with effort, his voice tremulous with emotion.

His mother's eyes grew wide, as did her mouth.

Nobody else noticed.

"Do not speak," he warned. "When next I come, prepare to run."

Then, with much reluctance, he walked away, and back to Vinny.

"I told her!" Ramose said, surprised by his success.

"Good goin', kiddo!"

"Now what will we do, Vinny?" asked Ramose anxiously.

"Now I gotta see a few pals."

"Friends?" shrieked Ramose. "At a time such as this?"

"*Especially* at a time such as this. Now, pay real close attention. Tomorrow, we return. Position yerself by the coffin, real casual. When ya sense the right moment, create a diversion—just like yer father used to. Then grab yer mother and scram."

"Do *what*?"

"Run!"

"But where will *you* be, Vinny?" asked Ramose. "I cannot do this alone! I can think of no distraction!"

"Then just snatch 'er. I'll be outside, waitin' to do my bit."

"Vinny, I cannot—" Ramose began.

"Don't worry. It's a piece o' cake, kiddo."

Outside, the sun had burned off the fog, warming up the world. The sky blazed, bluer than blue. Fountains gargled noisily. Everywhere, birds warbled their hearts out for joy, as Ramose and Vinny entered the park again.

Ramose looked around. He noticed things he had not seen before, worried sick as he had been about his mother. The whiteness called snow had almost completely departed. The dead trees were sprigging, sending out tiny green leaves, like bright green sleeves covering their branches. The great field shone with a tender tapestry of shoots. Nearly every shrub was budding. Nearly every space upon the ground burst with blooms.

"Look, Vinny!" he cried. "Leaves! Buds! Flowers!"

"Yeah, them's pussy willows an' crocuses an' snowdrops an' such—all yer first-comers."

"Coming to what?"

"Spring, the Great Renewal. Ain't it *grand*, kiddo?"

"Yes, it is," whispered Ramose. He had once known spring, but nothing like this.

"Now I'm gonna organize my buddies for tomorrow—when we spring yer mother," Vinny explained. "You remain here enjoyin' the flowers."

"Gladly," replied Ramose.

Vinny flew off. Ramose sat down upon a park bench. He closed his eyes, inhaling the scents of the many growing things—the unsettling smell he had noticed earlier, but could not identify—the aroma of life itself. He opened his eyes and enjoyed the great greenness and the brilliant colors of the season. The glory around him made Ramose feel better.

"Mother," he whispered into the flower-sweetened air, "this is spring. And tomorrow I shall spring you."

# XXI

# THE FAT LADY SINGS

JUST as on the morning before, Ramose and Vinny stood outside of the Central Museum, waiting for its doors to open. Ramose felt so nervous, he wanted to gnaw his fingernails, but he could not reach them, gold capped and swathed as they were. Instead, he picked a flower. Holding it helped him keep calm.

Suddenly, Vinny said, "OK, now ya swing into action. *Go!*"

"I am frightened, Vinny," Ramose said. "I still have no diversion."

"I've got confidence. You'll get a brainwave,

kiddo. Just don't forget ta pick up a button. I'll be waitin'. *Bone chance!"*

Ramose hesitated. Inside the museum, probably as nervous as he, his mother was most certainly waiting. *What if I fail?* he thought. *How I wish I were brave-hearted and daring, like Father.*

"You *can* do this," he told himself, screwing up his resolve. "You are one cool customer."

Then, standing as tall as a pharaoh of old, he strode into the New York Central Museum of Art—straight up to his mother.

"Stand back, little boy," said the man on guard. "You don't want to smother her," he joked lamely. "She's a treasure."

Ramose did not feel in the least like joking. Grave robbers had plundered his mother, and now this mindless horde stood gawping at her, making light of her predicament. Anger seethed inside him, like the hot heart of the gold workers' furnace. Ramose did not wish to harm these lovers of art, only to frighten them. His anger suddenly turned to brilliance.

"I am *not* a little boy!" he moaned in a spooky voice. "I am the Rabid Mummy! *You* stand back, or I shall smite you with my curse!"

Ramose began aping the actions of the movie mummy.

Most probably the guard had seen the same movie, for he gaped goggle-eyed at Ramose. "Help!" he jibbered, brandishing his keys. "Somebody save me!"

But nobody was *about* to do that. It seemed that everybody had seen the same film. The crowd began blithering, frozen in its tracks.

"The rabid mummy from the movie!"

"This is it, we're dead!"

"Good-bye, sweet world!"

While the crowd stood thunderstruck, in a splurge of strength Ramose lifted the glass that covered his mother and helped her from her coffin. Then, they ran for their lives.

Outside, as promised, Vinny was waiting—Vinny and thousands of his closest pals.

"FOR THE FAMILY!" squawked Vinny.

With a great phlumpetting of wings and a murmur like the purr of countless cats, the pigeons rose in a body. They surrounded Ramose and his mother, concealing them completely. In this way, they escaped.

"What's goin' on? Where'd these crazy birds come from?" yelled a man when the great flock swirled past.

His companion bellowed back, *Must be some weird migration!*

Apparently, the people in the museum decided that the coast was clear. The crowd streamed out, shrieking, and raced away. The guards streamed out, shrieking, and also raced away. Dr. Smythe, the mummy expert, streamed out. He did not race away.

"Stop those mummies! Our exhibit is escaping!" he shouted till he rasped.

But who could find them? The cloud of creatures was so thick, nobody could possibly see the mummies for the birds. As they dashed, Ramose began telling Vinny about his diversion.

But suddenly Ramose heard something. The sound of thudding feet. Right behind them. Somebody *else* was running inside the getaway flock! They were caught!

"NO-O-O-O-O!" Ramose wailed and screeched to a halt. "You can't have her!" He raised the hand that held the flower.

"Well, kill me with a crocus," said the pursuer.

Ramose gasped.

"Gerald!" he cried. "Quincy! Brandon! Hunter! Morgan! Oh, my goodness." He covered his face.

"I told you we nearly lived at the Central Museum," Gerald said. "Wow! What a super escape!"

By then the great flock of pigeons had settled like a gray sea to the sidewalk. Gerald looked past Ramose. "So," he asked respectfully, "is this your mother?"

Everything grew quiet. "Oh, my goodness! Mother—" Ramose said, turning around. Lovingly, Ramose and his mother gazed upon each other.

"My dear little duck," said his mother, clearly overcome.

Ramose whispered roughly, barely able to speak, *"Mother! Praise be!"*

Then they embraced tenderly.

"I knew you would come," said his mother.

"How?"

"Because I know you. Because you are my son."

Vinny waddled up.

"Mother, this is Vinny, my friend. These boys are also friends," Ramose said happily. "I could not have rescued you without them."

Ramose's mother smoothed her hair, done in Hathor style, which by then was quite disheveled.

"My thanks," she said, bowing graciously. In spite of the shabbiness of her wrappings, she was majestic in every way. "My thanks to *all* of you," she stated in her flutelike voice. "Should I hold some sway in the Afterlife, the pigeon will join the gods. And so will these five boys."

At that, all the birds fluttered and wigwagged their heads and cooed like mad. Vinny blushed. The boys' ears got red.

"It was nuthin', yer Highest-nest, just a little ca-moo-flage," Vinny said. "Anything to return your boy to his mom. Yer son pulled it off—with his special curse. He's gotta lotta moxie."

"What is that?" inquired Ramose's mother.

"Soda pop," explained Vinny. "But it also means courage."

"I am not brave," protested Ramose. "I did it for love."

"Love," Vinny mused, "the great power. Speakin' o' power, you'd a made a *great* pharaoh, kiddo!"

Ramose stared off into some dream place. He thought long and long, about the feat he had accomplished.

At last he said, "Perhaps I would have."

Joy danced inside Ramose's chest. His mother was free, he was free, and they were surrounded by friends.

Suddenly, the scream of sirens shredded the air.

Vinny said, "Here come the rampagin' hordes. Ya betta get goin'."

"I will not forget you," Ramose whispered. "Good-bye, again."

"Can't get rid of us that easily," Gerald said. "We'll help you find a ship."

"Good-bye, Vinny, my brother."

Vinny chuckled and with one wing wiped away a tear.

"Nice try, kiddo," he said. "But me and my pals're comin' too. We're your cover."

"What is this news that you are brothers?" asked Ramose's mother, rather surprised as they dashed along.

"I will explain it to you in time, Mother," said Ramose. "Now, I am taking you home."

# AUTHOR'S NOTE

WE all know that a four-thousand-and-ten–year-old mummy (or *any* mummy, for that matter) couldn't dash from his tomb, chat with a camel, and race off on a family quest. But once the idea struck me (at the Metropolitan Museum of Art in New York City), it was great fun to try to step inside the skin of a mummy boy and imagine how our world would seem to him.

I have been fascinated by Egypt since I read Richard Halliburton's *Complete Book of Marvels* in fifth grade. I wanted to see it for myself. In 1972, with my husband, I did. I rode camels, went inside the Great Pyramid, crouched in tombs to gawk at dazzling paintings of

Anubis, god of embalming, and Thoth, god of wisdom, saw far off what Ramose called the Land of Punt (Ethiopia), and drank coffee in a bedouin tent while the sun melted over the sands of Karnak.

Once, before dawn (because it's frizzling hot the moment the sun shows up), we trekked behind the Temple of Hatshepsut. There was nobody else around, but a bedouin boy, who popped from nowhere, wagging a dried-up hand to sell—"cheap." In the 1800s, a tourist craze was to lug an *entire* mummy home. Just a little souvenir. We somehow managed to control ourselves and left the hand behind. As we walked along, we found tiny faience (bright-colored clay) beads in the sand and whole sweeps of giant petrified clams. What a place— every inch! I stuffed as many memories of Egypt as I could into this book.

On another trip, I whacked my way into the Ping-Pong finals on the S.S. *France*, so I added that in, too. Golly! This is practically a true story!

You can read more about mummies and embalming, highly gripping (even to Vinny, the pigeon). And you might want to check out the Manchester Museum Egyptian Mummy Project online to find out how mummies help science and medicine.